Seeker

Volume 1

Azure Whitewood

SEEKER
AZURE WHITEWOOD

SEEKER
© AZURE WHITEWOOD 2019
First published in 2019.

ISBN-13 9781096788096

Prologue

The day Roger Persefall turned twenty, his life changed forever, unwillingly and cruelly. He had awoken as a Seeker.

The sun was burning down on the already dead grass. This year's summer was especially harsh. The farmers all over the territory were complaining about their crops falling victim to the heat. Roger Persefall had heard them all.

He was traveling for over five years now and a few years of that time in Astra, a king-ruled territory in the human realm that bordered the sea. The human realm consisted of several territories which were ruled by a royal family each. All had their own cities, towns and villages.

Roger had seen a lot during his five years and collected a fair share of knowledge. But it wasn't his choice to become a traveler, more a notion of fate. While he had many things in common with travelers, there was something different, the difference between mere travelers and Seekers.

Seekers awoke at the age of twenty. They didn't know about their fate ahead of time, nobody knew, but it could be bestowed upon anyone.

All awakened Seekers suddenly left the place they called home and went on a journey unknown to any other.

There was nothing they could do against it. Their inner nature compelled them to seek. They were driven to search for ancient spells, spells that suddenly appeared over 700 years ago together with the awakening of the first Seekers.

Those spells were bound to a location and invisible to the common man. Only a Seeker could reveal these spells but only one of them at a time. A Seeker knew where the next ancient spell resided. They felt it like a sixth sense.

When they reached it, they conducted a ritual in which they deciphered the ancient language of the spell until it eventually unleashed.

Only then the Seeker knew the consequences of the ancient spell. But that was where the danger came from. Ancient magic was powerful. It could bring great changes, were they blessings or calamities.

That was the reason Seekers were regarded as criminals. They did anything in their power to decipher a spell and when they did, the spell could be harmless or wipe out an entire city or bring forth even greater disaster.

There was no way the royal families would allow such a practice legally. That was why Roger had to live under disguise. He couldn't reveal the truth to anyone. He had to hide it deep inside, fooling the people around him. If he failed at that task, he'd be executed. But even if he wanted to stop, there was nothing he could do against his inner drives that made him a Seeker.

It meant a life of loneliness. It was a curse. But on the other side of the coin, a Seeker experienced what nobody else did. Still it was not an easy life.

But a Seeker wasn't lost in despair. There was a promised end to their journey. The ancient spell that was said to release them from their curse and reward them with a single yet omnipotent wish. It was ancient magic that had the potential to change the world. This mighty spell was commonly referred to as the Seeker's Dream.

Once a Seeker awakened, he gained the knowledge about what he needed to do and what the Seeker's Dream was. But for Roger this promised spell truly was a dream.

With an age of 25, he could have married a beautiful wife, have children and live together happily with his family. But Roger was just at the beginning of his journey and there was no end in sight.

There was no way to tell when he would find the Seeker's Dream and it even was uncertain if he was the chosen one. After all, he was just one of many Seekers. Perhaps even the knowledge he had been granted on his awakening was a lie. Perhaps there was no Seeker's Dream after all. But Roger believed that there was a purpose for Seekers to exist.

There was less known about Seekers. All knowledge about ancient magic was lost during the Great Purification War. A thousand years have passed since, and the calendar had changed from the year 3441 to 1131 post-purification, 1131 p.p. for short.

Civilization was almost wiped out during that war. Much of the technology back then was lost and so the knowledge about ancient magic.

It was the only form of magic all races could use. Now magic was exclusive to races like the elves. Humans, such as Roger, had to get by without the convenience of it. But being able to use magic or not was of no concern to Roger. His next goal was simply to conduct the ritual to decipher the ancient spell that was waiting for him in the town up ahead.

Roger was sitting on the distressing saddle of his horse and was eagerly looking forward to jump in one of the inns' beds and relieve his bottom of this torture. He had came a long way since he deciphered his last spell which had been in the distant east of Astra.

Bound to the saddle was a leather bag the size of his trunk that hopped up and down with the horse's trot. It contained everything he needed on his journey, belongings of a traveler and that of a Seeker. A knife, fire steel, food and water were necessities and the rest that was lurking at the bottom was equipment that was better kept away from the eyes of the curious.

He had just reached the top portion of a hill and was able to see the town up ahead. It was a spot of dozens of neatly packed buildings ranging from houses of the peasants to the sky-reaching church whose pointy tip stood out among all others.

Roger guessed that the town housed about a thousand souls. It looked like a fine town indeed. None of the buildings in his view had been forsaken and fallen to ruin, a sight he had encountered a number of times in the past. But especially because of the town's good shape, the surrounding fields made for a crucifying disparity.

Crops that threatened to crumble at any moment, or perhaps spark a flame, had Roger thinking about the winter that would arrive eventually. Perhaps if he returned in the following years, the town's picture would be painted differently. Living at the mercy of nature was cruel, but Roger wondered if he would exchange such a life for his current if he was presented the opportunity. Both were bitter in their own way.

Roger's thoughts were interrupted by a sudden and displeasing sound emerging from behind in the distance. It was the sound of wooden wheels clattering on the uneven ground.

He cast a glance backwards. It was a carriage painted in colorful luxuries. Undoubtably it was transporting some mighty nobleman.

Roger let out a sigh. He wasn't keen on nobility. They were particularly good at talking and worse at everything else. And since unlike the common man, they were high in rank, making them especially motivated to chide those that stood lower. The lower ranks better bent a knee if they preferred keeping their head where it was.

But especially since Roger was a Seeker, he needed to

be extra careful to abide by the common rules of treating nobility. Being captured and punished for a lack of manners was the least thing he desired, considering his already harsh condition of keeping his identity hidden.

Roger stopped his horse on a spot of grass next to the dirt road. He heard a faint crackling of the blades screaming for a change of weather.

He dismounted the horse, waiting patiently for the carriage to arrive. He paid special attention that neither his horse's nor his own feet were touching the road since it was entirely reserved for the mighty carriage coming his way.

With a hand to his heart, he bowed slightly as the carriage approached. He was full of hope that the nobleman had urgent matters to attend and would just continue his way without wasting a glance on him.

Roger held back a click of the tongue when he heard the bumping of the wheels quieting. The carriage had stopped, right in front of him. The driver stepped down and hurried swiftly to the door and opened it.

"Lord Gaynesford, if you might..."

A man more wide then tall slowly exited the carriage, his chest held high and a smug look on his face. His clothes were of fine silk, and his hat had a white feather attached to it pointing backwards.

"Well, well, what a bloody heat today is!" he said, comfortably scanning the environment.

His eyes wandered over the dry crops and put a satisfied smile in his face.

Roger was sure the man just imagined his hefty feasts in the winter, while the townspeople were eating but a potato a meal.

"Who do we have here? Raise your head!"

Roger did as he was told and rose his head.

"Yes, My Lord! It is an honor to meet you! I am but a humble merchant, Roger Persefall is my name," he said, repeating another bow.

"Persefall, huh? Never heard of that name before, ha-ha-ha!"

It took some time before his laughter quieted down. "Where're your goods?"

"I'll show them to you," Roger answered, turning his attention to his bag.

He opened it and took out a bundle of herbs.

Holding it in both hands, Roger offered the herbs for the nobleman to inspect. "Freshly picked herbs, My Lord."

"Herbs you say?" the man encountered, rising an eyebrow. "In this bloody heat? Impossible! What sorcery did you use?"

He sounded almost like accusing him of a crime, but Roger kept calm and replied.

"In the forest, if you look at the right places, you'll find an abundance."

The man looked at him doubtfully, but then his expression changed.

"Ha! A fine merchant you are! My name is Lewis Gaynesford, the great viscount of Strosa! These surely will fetch a high price," he declared, grinning widely.

Roger didn't like it. He cursed himself for encountering a viscount on his way. A viscount was even worse than a mere member of nobility. He ruled over a city and its surrounding land. People with this much power were particularly troublesome.

"I'm delighted to hear that, Lord Gaynesford."

The viscount's commendations meant nothing to him. He would sell those herbs to the town in reach to fool the people into thinking that he was an actual merchant. He couldn't care less for making money in a big city. Money had no value to him. All he needed was to reach the next spell and conduct the ritual.

"You are in luck today, merchant!" the viscount decided, showing his teeth. "I've witnessed your skills," he continued, passing on the bundle to his driver who then stored it inside the carriage.

"I'll be taking these as prove."

The nobleman had just stolen Roger's goods. There were no doubts that the man was driven by his own greed.

"If I may, My Lord… a merchant needs his goods to survive," Roger said, trying to appeal to the viscounts sense of guilt.

That's why he hated nobility. They were a greedy bunch and would go as far as robbing the common man in law's name.

"Merchants are as greedy as they say… isn't there another bundle in your bag? Surely you can survive with that," the viscount spit out, disgusted.

If Roger didn't have an urgent reason to avoid even the smallest trouble, he would have punched him on the spot. But he stayed calm, to the outside at least.

"It's truly as you say, My Lord!"

Roger had no choice but to play submissive. Overstepping his bounds could lose him a lot more than just a bundle of herbs. He let the viscount greed them, as long as he left quickly, Roger thought.

"Wise decision, merchant," the nobleman encountered, entering the carriage, barely making it back inside. "Driver!" he shouted rudely.

The driver jumped on his words, getting in position to close the door.

Once inside, the viscount turned and said his final words.

"Farewell, merchant. If we see each other again, I expect another lot of excellent goods!"

His face vanished inside the carriage, and the driver closed the door. Then he quickly sprinted to the front and drove off.

Roger remained on the grass as his eyes followed the carriage shrinking in the distance.

That's why Roger hated nobility.

"Curse them!" he murmured to himself after the carriage had put enough distance between them.

Not only was Roger legally robbed of half of his herbs, he also would be arriving late in Spirithelm. That was the name of the town up ahead.

Even if he wanted to go faster to take back the lost time, he couldn't pass the carriage since this was a thing one simply could not do.

But Roger had to look at this from a brighter angle. He didn't really care about the herbs. He just needed to make the impression that he was a real merchant. The townspeople would get wary of visitors with unclear intentions, and wariness was the last thing he needed as a Seeker. His remaining bundle would be more than enough to accomplish that task.

After waiting for some time, Roger mounted his horse and continued towards Spirithelm. The ancient spell was waiting, or it was more accurate to say it was impatiently drawing him closer. It wasn't the same as seeing it, but he knew exactly where the spell was. From the hilltop it appeared to be inside the church.

He needed to conduct the ritual over night since being seen would be the end of him. The church was locked at night, but lock security was weak in these times and he was properly equipped. Without decent lock picking skills, he wouldn't have come this far.

Surely a Seeker could spend their whole life trying to decipher their first spell, but since they were driven by their inner nature, they attempted everything possible to successfully decipher it. And that ensured that Seekers had a wide range of skills tailored towards reaching and deciphering ancient spells.

Of course, deception was on of them. The viscount was fully convinced that Roger was a merchant and there was no way around it. A Seeker's skill of imitation was perfect. Perhaps that was one of the good sides of being a Seeker. They never gave up on improving their skills if it helped them decipher spells.

Chapter 1

Roger had come a good way since he encountered the viscount and the town was at his feet. The first thing he needed to do was to visit the local market and make sure that people recognized him as a proper merchant.

He had just entered town and saw a woman carrying a basket of potatoes into her house.

He stopped his horse.

"Madam, may I ask you for where the market lies?" he asked, showing her a friendly smile.

She turned around.

"Oh, surely! Follow the road and head left by the church!"

"I am in your debt." Roger said, politely lowering his head.

The woman turned back around and vanished behind the door.

Roger set his horse into motion and followed her

directions.

Along the road were a number of houses belonging to the peasants of Spirithelm. The closer he rode to the center, the more stores and other public buildings had replaced them.

Then he reached a wide place with a well in the middle. Behind it was the mighty church the woman spoke of. It stretched far to the heavens. This was without a doubt the place where the spell resided. He could feel the glow of it inside.

But he had to be careful not to get too close. When a Seeker went near his next ancient spell, it reacted and became visible to the common eye.

Ancient spells were composed of a magic circle with complex forms and ancient signs describing the nature of the spell. He couldn't understand ancient language, but as a Seeker he had the ability to grasp its meaning the moment he had fully deciphered it.

He turned left as the woman said. The only other option was turning right which would lead him out of town to the north.

The road led further into the town center. The houses now had been mostly replaced with stores and market stands. And then he arrived at a huge plaza with lots of people swarming around. He had found the marketplace. Now he just needed to make an impression and sell his herbs.

"Excuse me! Where can I sell some herbs?" Roger asked the muscular man behind the stand closest to him.

On his table were lots of shimmering crystals, chains and other glamorous things. If Roger had met this man on the open street, he would never have guessed that he was selling such things.

"Oh? Herbs you say? In this heat? They are in high demand I've heard," the stand owner said, pointing at the other end of the plaza.

Roger bowed his head in gratitude and made his way through the masses.

There weren't many merchants around and especially no one who sat on a horse. However, this was to the advantage of Roger. This way the townspeople would surely recognize him as a fine merchant. After all, a merchant wouldn't carry his goods by hand.

He arrived at the herb stand.

Although it was unmistakably a stand selling herbs, the number of them was quite sparse and they reminded him more of the crops outside of town than those in his bag. But that was naturally due to the harsh summer. The stand owner had to be careful the herbs didn't catch fire all of the sudden.

She was a slim woman standing behind her stand, crossing her arms. She was chewing on a straw. Roger immediately knew that she was in this business for quite some time.

He unmounted his horse and took the herbs from his bag, half the amount he originally intended to sell, but luckily the viscount didn't demand all of them.

He walked over to the stand and presented the bundle to her.

She looked at it with wide eyes.

"What is this?" she gasped, her straw falling from her mouth. "Where did you find them?"

"Deep in the forests to the east. In places where the

woods are thick, you'll find an abundance of plants being protected from the heat."

"Oh? But it couldn't have been easy to obtain them… I haven't seen herbs this fresh since last year."

Roger just smiled at her comfortably.

For him it was quite easy to obtain them. As a Seeker he needed a good understanding of his environment. Especially forests were a good place for many predicaments, like losing chasers, finding food or taking shelter from the weather. However, most people wouldn't consider going too deep into forests. There were monsters lurking in the trees and caves, and it could become life threatening very quickly. But Roger had encountered too many of those threats to be afraid. He knew their behavior and weaknesses. And if the monsters came to him, they spared him the trouble of looking for food.

The herb woman turned around to the back and rummaged through a small bag made of cloth. When she turned back around, she showed her open hand to Roger. He counted five silver coins.

"What do you say? I think five silvers is a reasonable price for such quality herbs," the woman declared with a smile.

And it was true. Five silver coins were quite reasonable, but Roger also knew how business as a merchant worked.

"Make it six and it's a deal," Roger encountered, showing his best merchant smile. Roger knew that stand owners always were prepared to raise the price a bit.

She smiled back at him and added another silver coin she had hidden in her other hand. There was no need for them to say anything about this farce. That was just business as usual. One could tell a fine merchant from an amateur by observing their response to initial price offerings.

"It was a pleasure to do business with you," Roger said in a plain voice.

It was a common phrase to say after finalizing a deal. There was no need to get emotional over it. He stretched out his hand and the woman gave him the coins. And he gave her the bundle of herbs and the deal was done.

Roger mounted his horse while she was admiring the freshness of the herbs she just bought. She put the bundle under her stand, perhaps to protect it from the heat. He wouldn't be surprised if she took those home and used them herself. After all, it was a rare opportunity this summer.

Roger saw her taking another straw from below and put it in her mouth. She assumed her earlier pose crossing arms and started chewing.

He then searched for another stand that sold silver oil. It was easily flammable and had loyally assisted him in the past. The oil was extracted out of the leaves of silver acacia trees. The oil had a silver and shiny color, therefore the name.

Once he found the right stand, he bought three skins of it since he had used up most of his reserves.

Roger then turned his horse around and headed back the way he came from. He had already seen an inn on the way. It was a large building surrounded by stores and even had a stable, a common addition to most inns. After all, travelers make most of the customers. He placed his horse in the stables and entered. Naturally he had his bag with him. Leaving it in the stable was asking for theft.

The inside was mostly made out of wood. There weren't any dusty corners nor lurking spiders in sight as he had seen in some other inns in the past. It was a quite welcome init.

There were tables and benches around for people to eat. One didn't need to rent a room to enjoy a meal, so especially in the evening such places tended to become very lively.

Roger headed straight to the man behind the counter. He stood there like a bear, raising the question how he got inside. Roger assumed that this inn was a quite peaceful spot. No one, even drunk, would cause any commotion if that man was standing there.

"One room for the night," Roger said, putting a silver coin on the wooden counter.

The man just took the coin and put one of the keys from the wall in its place.

"Room number three, right up the stairs," he said in a flat voice.

Roger couldn't tell what the man was thinking. He just quietly took the keys and headed to the mentioned stairs.

He was delighted that they seemed to be in good shape. The last thing he needed was the sound of old stairs giving way when he sneaked out during the night.

He headed to the upper floor and stopped in front of the door with the number three engraved in the wood.

He took a glimpse at the keys. It wasn't an unfamiliar view. He hadn't encountered many locks in his five years of traveling that were safe. He had the tools in his bag that allowed him to get past most he encountered.

The best way to ensure nobody entered without permission was hiring guards. But those were only reserved for high and mighty noblemen. Roger was sure the viscount from earlier was no exception.

He unlocked the door. The room was held simple with just a wooden bed in the corner and a window with some wooden covers to keep out the wind.

He put his bag on the bed and sat himself next to it. Before he could proceed with his plans for the night, he needed to wait for it to arrive.

He closed his eyes and felt a glowing light in the distance, the spell. He wondered what would await him there. So far he had been in luck. None of the spells he had deciphered had caused major disasters like he had heard of. But at the same time he was looking forward to uncovering its secrets. He opened his eyes again.

The light shone through the window cover and illuminated the room gently. He noticed some dust glittering in the sun rays.

Then he remembered the tiredness from his long travel to Spirithelm. He took his shoes off and laid himself on the bed and closed his eyes again.

He rested until the evening. The sun would vanish beneath the roofs any moment.

He went downstairs to eat in the tavern below. After all, he would spend half of the night doing his ritual. He needed enough strength.

When he came down from the stairs, he saw that the number of people filled his expectations. It wasn't yet time for local drinkers to arrive, but merchants and travelers from all over were gathered at the tables, talking.

Roger sat himself on an empty seat.

"One serving roasted pork please," he told one of the serving wenches.

Quite some time later the girl brought him his food. He paid for it and readied himself for the feast. He spent more money than usual for the meal, but he had made quite some money today with his herbs and the night awaiting him was long. He couldn't remember how long it had been since he had a proper meal.

He eyed the juicy-looking pork in front of him and took knife and fork. Its sweet fragrant entered his nose and the sensation spread through his body like a wave.

He dove his knife into the meat and began to eat. Like an explosion the taste of the seasoning and the wild filled his mouth on his first bite. He felt like his body was gently wrapped in the tender pork. He quickly took the next bite and another one.

As he savored his dish, a man sat himself across the table.

"A beer," he shouted to one of the girls, throwing her a lustful expression.

Then he turned to Roger.

"Ya, fella'! Hope ya' don't mind me here."

Roger could tell immediately that he was one of the local farmers.

"If you don't mind, I don't mind," Roger answered plainly.

The farmer smiled at Roger showing him his damaged teeth.

"This flamin' summer heat… my crops are dead. I ain't know how this will end," he wailed, frowning.

Roger concluded that he was in a financial crisis. And the solution for most of those people was alcohol. And that was the moment the girl brought him his foaming beer. The man leaned over to her in an attempt to get her to fall for him, but the girl hurriedly took her leave. Defeated, he turned to his beer and in one fine swoop emptied out half of it.

"Waaahhh…" he breathed out.

Roger realized that he didn't have any more time to enjoy his meal. If he didn't hurry, he could get caught up in this drunkard's foolish actions. Roger quickly took another bite.

The farmer eyed him.

"Oh, flamin' summer heat… and my wife is giving me an earful about it…" He continued rattling on while supporting his head with his hand. His eyes followed the foam inside his mug drifting around in circles.

"Truly. The summer heat is not well-becoming, but fall is hurrying in large steps," Roger assured him.

He had to keep up the conversation until he had finished eating. Ignoring such a man would only cause him further trouble.

But he didn't listen to Roger's words.

"I'm sure the heat is the work of one those damned Seekers," he complained angrily, clenching his teeth in anger. "They're making me suffer!"

Roger kept his reactions to himself. He cut off another piece of pork and put it in his mouth.

It was common that people blamed their problems on Seekers. They couldn't blame it on god without risking their head, nor on themselves since it wouldn't become their fragile hearts very well.

However, Roger was sure he wasn't inclined to listen to the man badmouthing him to his face. He took the last bite and put knife and fork on the empty plate.

"Sorry, I have to excuse myself here," Roger said, rising.

Roger quickly left the man where he was and hurried up the stairs.

The drunkard's reactions were already too delayed to find a response quick enough.

Roger went to his room and prepared for the night.

He didn't need to take a look to know what type of lock the church used. It was the same all over the territory. All he needed were his skeleton keys, convenient tools that allowed him to open most of the locks around.

He waited until night had arrived and the moon was up high.

Then it was time he sneaked out of the inn. Getting seen walking out of the inn at midnight would only raise suspicion, so he needed to be extra careful. But he knew that even bears needed their night's sleep, so he had no trouble of exiting the inn without being asked uncomfortable questions.

Before he opened the door to exit the inn, he put on his black mantle to become one with the darkness of the night. It allowed him to remain unrecognized even if someone saw him. With a big hood it shielded his face from any curious onlookers. However, the mantle itself was cause for suspicion, so he still needed to stay unseen.

Roger carefully opened the wooden door, not to make any noise, and exited the inn. He looked around a few times making sure nobody was in sight.

With large but quiet steps he hurried to the church. The faster he could hide within, the less chance he had to be spotted.

Eventually, he stood before it. He lifted the metal lock with his hand and went through his skeleton keys and tried them out one by one. It didn't take him long before he had found the right one and the lock snapped open.

He opened the door slowly and carefully put his head between the gap to look inside. It was dark but a bit of moonlight shone through the mosaic windows of glass that reached to the top of the building.

He stepped inside and closed the door behind him. He could feel the ancient spell that was right before him. It was placed at the front near the altar.

He took a few steps through the pathway between the benches.

The spell reacted.

A magic circle with complex forms and signs appeared in a bright, bluish glow and covered the back of the church as well as the first rows of benches. Roger felt the intense power it emitted.

He walked to the front until he stood before the altar, near the center of the magic circle. Then he closed his eyes.

Complex forms and signs unbeknownst to him entered his mind, piece by piece. He couldn't understand any of it, but as a Seeker he would understand eventually.

Deciphering an ancient spell could take anywhere

from a few hours to days. The process could be interrupted and continued at any time without losing progress. The time it took to decipher a spell depended on the Seeker's experience. And the more ancient language he had absorbed, the easier it was to take in more.

Luckily, this ancient spell was in a church that was closed at night. He could conduct the ritual in one single night. If it were in a palace swarming with guards, not only would it be incredibly hard to enter without notice, it also would be necessary to decipher a bit of the spell on many different days. More so, since the spell became visible to the common eye if the Seeker went near it.

A Seeker needed to make sure that absolutely no one was nearby. Otherwise the chances of concluding the ritual without getting caught were slim at best and being caught followed a cruel ritual designated to Seekers only.

But Roger was not in such an unfortunate situation. He had enough time to finish before sunrise. Nobody would ever notice that he did. Then he would simply leave Spirithelm and continue his way to the next spell. That was a Seeker's fate.

Several hours had passed. Just a few minutes were remaining until Roger had grasped the nature of the spell.

The complex shapes and signs were streaming through his mind at incredible speed. Whenever he conducted the ritual, he somehow felt very relaxed. He felt as light as if disconnected from the world around him.

Then his relaxation turned into anticipation. Only a

few hundred signs were left. It was like his body urged him forward to take the last sprint. He couldn't await to discover the secret behind the spell.

Then his eyes flashed open. He was done. The ritual was complete. He had grasped the nature of the spell.

"...a seal?"

The lines of the magic circle around him started glowing in a bright red.

It was a powerful spell that would lift a seal in the coming moments, but he didn't know what had been sealed here and when. He only knew that it was something that had been sealed with the most powerful magic that ever existed.

Right in front of him a gate of light opened from the ground. He quickly took a few steps to the side, but it wasn't enough. His body drove him further, close to the church's wall. A shiver ran down his back. His mind was focused on the contents of the seal. He stared at the concentrated mass of light in the center.

Then something started emerging from the ground. It was pitch black as if it swallowed all the light around it. Slowly something raised from the ground, revealing the body of a female figure. It was her hair that was pitch black.

She had emerged up to her hips, but the hair still didn't end. Roger was captivated by the sight. He couldn't move. An ominous aura originated from the girl.

Then the lines of the magic circle started dissolving inwards and eventually the spell disappeared, leaving no trace of its existence. All prove that was left was the mysterious figure.

The moment the girl turned her head towards him,

his heart stopped beating for what felt like an eternity.

The being that was sealed here was beyond everything he had seen in his entire 25 years he lived. Her eyes were glowing a deep red. They reminded him of thick blood. Her black hair that reached below her knees made her eyes appear even more fearsome. She wasn't human. From her back grew small, black, feathered wings, and below a black, thin hairless tail with a heart-shaped tip wove around, reflecting the moonlight.

Roger's body told him to run. But there was no way he could escape.

Then his arms moved on their own. He grabbed the knife from his bag and held it tightly with his shacking hands.

The girl's body slowly started moving. She raised her foot and turned towards him.

Then his vision went black. An ear-shattering sound rang through his head. He felt a hard sensation on his back that quickly turned into stinging pain. The air in his lung exited forcefully.

When he opened his eyes again, he stared into an endless sea of red. Her eyes filled his entire gaze. He couldn't budge his own.

"Human!"

Her voice seized his entire body.

"Speak the year!"

"1131," Roger answered instantly.

Roger could see her big eyes widen. Then she moved her head away and assumed an upright posture, her eyes cast down on him.

Now that Roger had a clear sight of her full body, he noticed that she didn't have any clothes. She looked like a twelve year-old human girl. A girl that had just entered the age for marriage. But with her eyes, wings and tail she was undeniably inhuman. She was a demon. A race that was said to have become extinct over a thousand years ago.

"Is this the past...?" the girl murmured to herself, casting her eyes to her side.

She appeared a lot less fearsome than moments ago.

"Human, did you lift my seal?" she continued, gazing at him.

Roger's muscles had stopped tensing up. He could move again. However, upon moving his back away from the wall, he felt it aching, but there didn't seem to be anything broken. He looked up to her.

"I did."

Without moving her gaze, she asked, "Is it the truth? The year is 1131?"

For a moment Roger felt a glimpse of fear in her voice. His own senses must have been dulled by the impact. The demon in front of him didn't make the impression to be capable of feeling this emotion.

"It is. The year is 1131," Roger said calmly.

The demon girl's eyes became unsteady. She almost looked like she was worried, but was that even possible? According to what he heard about them, they were living manslaughterers. Nobody could escape their blood-lust. But thankfully, the blood-lust he felt earlier had disappeared. Perhaps tomorrow, he could tell proudly that he survived an encounter with a demon, not that he had anyone to boast to.

She interrupted his thoughts.

"Why is it that you tried to threaten me with a simple

blade?"

Her red eyes still felt like they were piercing his soul.

"I apologize if that seemed lacking respect. My hands moved on their own. I've never seen a demon before."

"Ha?!" she cried out as if he had said something unbelievably stupid. "Never met a demon? Are you jesting me?"

Roger's mouth continued to stand open thinking of the right words. He had to be careful not to anger her accidentally. That could be the very end of him.

"I may assure you I'm not," he answered with utmost seriousness.

She stumbled back a few steps. He could feel a different emotion from her. Was it disgust? He wasn't sure, but he could feel her resentment.

Her arms dropped down seemingly losing all of their strength.

"Where is this place?" she asked, resting her head on her neck.

"This is a church in Astra, a territory in the Alurona realm."

"A-Alurona, you say?! That should have been laid to waste..."

"...to waste?" Roger echoed, frightened.

He had no doubt that her race would be capable of it.

"While I was sealed, came the war to an end?" she asked, somehow looking sincere.

The last war that involved demons was the last one of their race. It ended over a thousand years ago. She couldn't possibly have been sealed here for over a thousand years, could she? But when Roger thought of possible explanations, he couldn't come up with another one. The girl in front of him had slept for over a millennium. Her race was gone.

Roger was sure that until he completed the deciphering ritual there was no demon alive. But this changed with the girl standing in front of him. She was the sole survivor of a race that ceased to exit long before he was born. And she didn't seem to be aware of it.

She was a demon, an inhuman being, feared for generations, but still his heart was about to split in two. He couldn't imagine being in her position and how he would react.

Roger slowly stood up, dust falling from his clothes. When he looked behind him, he saw a huge crater around him. The sturdy church wall had been crushed halfway in. Without a doubt she was inhuman.

He turned towards her and looked in her deep, red-glowing eyes. She watched him uneasily, waiting for his words to clear her confusion. He spoke with utmost seriousness.

"The war you speak of… it ended in 3441 of the old calendar."

"3441, you say? That's the year I remember…"

She took back another step.

"The calendar changed after that. The war that was later to be named the *Great Purification War* had come to a close 1131 years ago."

"Pu-purification?"

She took back another two steps.

Roger didn't think it was possible, but the girl in front of him was engulfed in fear. And he knew the reason. The word purification meant the killing of demons. Roger didn't want to be in the position to tell her, but he considered it too cruel to leave it up for interpretation.

"When the war ended, the demon race ended with it. That's why I never saw a demon before today."

Roger observed the girl collapsing to her knees. Her eyes were wide open and she didn't move further. Her lower lip was shaking.

"This can't be..." she whispered with a breathy voice.

Roger could hear her voice clearly. There was no other sound present in this quiet night.

Moments later he could see the red light of her eyes being swallowed up by darkness. Her eyes closed slowly and she fell forward. With a dull sound her head hit the ground. She didn't move after that.

Roger was clueless for what to do. A demon that shouldn't exist, a said manslaughterer, was lying before him.

He carefully took a few steps closer. He saw some black feathers from her wings scattered across the ground. She must have lost them when she emerged from the seal.

He took another few steps and looked down on her body. She looked helpless. Her long hair covered her entire body. Her tail surfaced from under the sea of hair. It lay flat on the ground.

Suddenly he heard a creaking sound disrupting the silence of the night. His head snapped towards the church door.

Someone was there. He couldn't let himself be seen. Running from knights of the entire kingdom would be his end. Hastily he looked around searching for a way out of this situation.

When his eyes wandered over the crushed wall, he was reminded that it was impossible to cover up what happened here.

The church's walls were sturdy. Normally it would block all sounds to the outside. But when the girl crushed the wall earlier, the sound was similar to an explosion. If someone lived nearby, such as the priest, he would surely notice.

He saw his knife lying a fair distance away from the crushed wall. He didn't realize he had dropped it.

With quick steps he ran towards the knife and put it in his bag. He couldn't do anything about the wall, but he could escape from here. Nobody would ever know he had been in here.

However, he needed to leave Spirithelm immediately before the knights came to question people about the incident. Especially travelers were at risk of being suspected. If anyone saw him leaving the inn previously this night, it wouldn't take long to figure out that it was him, even if he was concealed under his black mantle.

The creaking sounds emerged again. Roger saw the door opening slowly.

He sprinted towards the benches to hide from the priest. But then he saw the girl lying on the floor that he had almost forgotten. He didn't consider her in his plans.

If the priest found the unconscious demon on the floor, he would know a Seeker was involved. It was no question that the demon race had perished. If one of those demons suddenly appeared again, it would be undoubtably the work of ancient magic. And the only ones that could unleash ancient spells were Seekers. The priest undoubtably would come to this conclusion.

Whenever a Seeker appeared somewhere, a huge search party of knights was cast forth. It was tough escaping them.

Roger changed his course towards the girl. He picked her up carefully, still wary, and hid behind the benches next to the wall.

She was surprisingly light. Her body was slender and her wings were as feathery as they looked. With his back to one of the benches, he waited for the priest to enter.

The creaking sounds came to an end. It was followed by careful footsteps, one after another. The sounds came closer. Roger's heart was racing. He had the cover of the dark, but if on the off-chance he was spotted, he wouldn't have a way out.

"Oh, great lord…"

The unbelieving voice of the priest replaced his footsteps.

Roger took his chance and slowly moved towards the church door.

When he had reached the last row of benches just before the exit, he slowly lurked towards the door.

Carefully he looked around the corner of the bench. The priest was standing in front of the crushed wall. Roger took his chance and left through the half-open door.

From there he entered the shadows of side alleys between the houses and ran towards the inn. The demon girl was still unconscious. He didn't know what to do with her, but the best option for him was to take her with him.

If he left her somewhere around here and she got found, he would be in deep trouble. He needed to be far away from Spirithelm before he could leave her behind.

He had reached the road of the inn. He was between two houses and carefully looked around the corner but couldn't see anyone.

Then he heard a turmoil emerging from the direction of the church. The priest must have notified the guards. He needed to hurry.

He ran towards the stables and untied the rein of his horse. Then he put the girl on the horse's back and led the horse to the road.

It wasn't exactly gallant to transport a girl that way, but he had no choice, and perhaps, human manners didn't apply to demons.

He mounted his horse and scourged the rein forcefully. The horse started running. Roger headed along the road that led away from the church.

He passed the marketplace that looked almost ghostly during this night. The lively atmosphere, the people and goods were gone. It was just an empty place that glistened in the cold moonlight.

He continued down the road. It didn't take him long until he had left Spirithelm. It was a small town after all.

Roger rode along the dirt road for several minutes until he got close to a forest. The trees were sparse and the ground solid.

He carefully guided his horse through. After a while he stopped at a small clearance just wide enough for a handful of people to fit.

He was deep enough into the forest that it was unlikely he'd be found by tomorrow. He hoped the guards would brush it off as just another unresolved incident, the will of god, perhaps.

Roger jumped from his horse and carefully removed the girl from its back. He carried her to a nearby tree and leaned her upper body against the rough bark.

He looked at her and realized that he couldn't leave her like that. He took off his black mantle, pulled her upper body away from the bark and put it around her. Even if she was a demon, he couldn't leave a girl naked in the forest.

Despite the hot day, in the night, it could become quite cold. He walked around to search for some suitable logs he could use for a campfire and piled them up neatly in the middle of the clearance.

He opened his bag and pulled out a skin with some leftover silver oil and poured it onto the logs.

It was a reliable method to ignite a fire. Even when it was raining, he could confidently start a fire with it. The heat from the burning oil drove out the water from the wet logs and eventually they caught fire as well. Any raindrops that made it through leaf cover sparked the flame anew.

He took his fire steel and the knife from his bag. The steel had about the size of his forearm which allowed it to produce strong and hot glowing sparks. He pointed it towards the oil-drenched logs. With his knife he slowly slid across the steel several times. Each time, the sparks were flying further until finally reaching the logs, igniting them.

The oil caught fire quickly and after some time the logs started burning as well. The warm flickering flame emitted a gentle shine on the nearby trees.

Roger now also sat down and leaned against another

tree.

Across the flame he could see the light flickering on her face. She looked almost innocent if he didn't know about her true nature.

He closed his eyes and took a deep breath to relax.

It had been an eventful night. He didn't know how things would continue. He had to somehow deal with the demon girl. And if things came to worse, he would need to move in the shadows if a search party was sent out.

But even if the wall of the church was crushed, there wasn't any indicator that a Seeker had been involved. He had taken his knife and the girl.

There was nothing left behind as evidence. Roger felt better after convincing himself of this.

He opened his eyes again, but he wasn't the only one.

The girl on the other side looked rather sleepy, having hers open just a tiny bit.

She had slept for over a thousand years. It wouldn't be surprising if that had any side effects on her body. She slowly raised her head, gazing at the flame.

Roger carefully observed her.

Then her eyes sprang open as she fully awoke. She looked at Roger. Her eyes had lost their red glow. They now were very dark, but they didn't seem odd. They could be mistaken as those of a human. It wasn't common to see someone with such dark eyes, but he had seen a few over the years.

The girl had been staring at Roger for quite some time now, just as when he first met her this night. She seemed to like staring at other people.

Her mouth went open for a moment but closed right after. She seemed to have difficulty finding the right words.

"I'm Roger Persefall. It might be a bit late for introductions, but odd twists of fate bring forth odd actions."

"Why did you—"

"Won't you tell me your name first?" he interrupted her gently.

She leaned forward and placed her hands on the ground as support. She chased the flame with her eyes.

"Liliesh Zeka Elralloth Ariestyse Erthroriach." She looked at him with a weak teasing smile. "Might be too much for a human to remember."

And indeed it was. He had lost her at the second.

"Liliesh Zeka El..." Roger began, struggling to remember. "You're right, it might be a bit long for me," he said, admitting his defeat.

The demon girl let out a laugh, but somehow it didn't seem as happy as a laugh should be.

"You really don't know my name... this truly is a thousand years in the future..." she said, lowering her clouded face.

"Are you saying humans knew your name back then?"

She forced a smile.

"Perhaps this is my fate... I lost the war... I couldn't protect my own race," she muttered and sunk her lonely gaze into the flames.

As the last remaining demon, she felt responsible for the demise of her race, Roger thought.

"The war wasn't your responsibility. There no need to blame yourself."

"Ha? What does a human know? You don't even know who I am!" she cried out, giving him a sharp look.

Roger flinched.

He was reminded to be careful with her. After he escaped the church, getting killed by the last remaining demon would be a surprising turn of fate he did not long for.

"I apologize. I don't know who you are."

"Truly you don't. Despicable!" She turned her head swiftly to the side.

Did he make her angry?

Roger decided to stay quiet. He couldn't risk making it worse.

After a while she stood up and walked closer. She stood right across the campfire and pointed her finger at him.

"Behold! I, Liliesh Zeka Elralloth Ariestyse Erthroriach, am the last remaining queen of the demon race, a foolish queen that let her race die. Remember this!"

Roger didn't find the words. She was a queen? Ruler of the demon race? The girl in front of him led the war against the allied races and had lost everything?

Roger took a moment to gather himself.

"I apologize for my rudeness towards a queen," he said calmly, lowering his head politely.

"Are perhaps all humans like this? Your words have no meaning!" she said angrily. She sat herself down. "I won't kill you. Don't pretend! Say how foolish I am!"

Roger was surprised that she saw through him. But he was confident in his farce. Over all the years there had been no one that saw through his lies. And the first one that did... was a demon?

"Why didn't you leave me behind? Surely it wasn't out of sympathy."

Roger avoided her gaze and looked at his hands, the same hands that carried her unconscious body out of the church.

"You're right. I did it because it was a rational choice, not because of noble intentions."

"See? You can speak honestly! But why was it rational to bring a demon with you?"

Roger let out a sarcastic chuckle.

"Your war surely messed things up! Seekers have replaced demons as the most feared existence... and I am one of those. If the priest had found a demon in the church, there would have been no doubt that a Seeker was involved," he blurted out, leaking some of the despair he had amassed over the years.

"You're the most feared existence? Ha! Ha-ha-ha!" She stood up and spun around, laughing. "How far humanity has fallen!"

Then she stopped turning and faced Roger again.

"So, what are you? What is a Seeker?"

Roger looked in her dark eyes.

"Anyone can become a Seeker, but it is not your choice to make. I awoke as a Seeker the day of my twentieth birthday. That was five years ago. Knowledge had been implanted in me, and I knew what I had to do. I had to travel to the ancient spell I could sense and decipher it."

"Ancient magic, you say..." she murmured to herself.

Roger realized that she had to know something about

the spells. Much information about that time was lost now, but she truly lived during those years.

"Do you know anything about it?"

She covered her lips with her curled fingers and seemed to be deep in thought. Then after a while she spoke up.

"I believe it was discovered just before the war started. The first to learn it were humans, but I don't know much about it. Apparently it was magic that could be wielded by all races."

Roger was surprised that even she, a demon queen that lived a thousand years ago, didn't know much about this magic.

"But weren't you sealed using ancient magic? The ancient spell in the church did lift your seal after all."

She looked at him in surprise.

"That was ancient magic you say?"

She appeared to be in thought again. Her face tensed up.

It seemed like she tried to remember something. Didn't she know how she was sealed?

"Say, what happens now after you used the spell?" she asked, interrupting his thoughts.

She looked at him, waiting for an answer. The tips of the flames raised between them.

"I have to wait three days until I know the location of the next spell."

"How many spells are there?" she asked shortly after.

She continued staring at him. Perhaps, this demon girl really showed interest in him, a human. But that seemed rather uncharacteristic.

"I don't know. Nobody knows."

"Ha?" she let out, almost falling backwards. "You don't know? Then when does it end?"

"There is an end, but I don't know if I will reach it. A spell referred to as Seeker's Dream is said to free Seekers from their curse."

"Seeker's Dream, you say? What is it? What will happen if you reach it?" she asked, continuing her stare.

He returned his eyes to the flame.

"It grants any wish, just one. But I don't know if it's true. This was in my head one day," he answered, remembering the day when his life as a Seeker began.

"Any wish…" she muttered, appearing to be in thoughts again.

Her gesture had sparked Roger's curiosity. She seemed to be thinking about the wish.

"If it were yours to make, what would you wish for?" he asked, interrupting her thoughts this time.

It didn't take long before she answered.

"I want to save my race."

Her eyes conveyed seriousness, not a shred of doubt.

"Then what are you going to do from now on?"

"I want to search for survivors of my kind. If I have survived, there have to be others," she said in a quiet voice.

Roger was convinced that she was the only one remaining. He couldn't imagine that any other demon had been sealed the same way. She was special, a queen, ruler of the demon race. He didn't know why or how she was sealed, but there had to be a reason. But he didn't want to tell her his thoughts. If she believed there were others, then so was it.

He felt as his eyes were getting heavier. He had spent a lot of energy for the ritual.

"Can we continue this after some sleep? I'm tired," he said, pausing for a moment. "Do demons even sleep?"

There was no answer. The girl quietly stared at the flame.

"Hey! You!" he called awkwardly. "Liliesh Zeka..." He attempted to remember her name.

"Lili is fine," she announced, releasing him from his struggles. "It's a human name, isn't it?"

Calling a demon queen Lili felt a bit unfit, but if she was fine with it, he'd call her that.

"Lili then. Do demons sleep?"

"Of course, we do! What do you think we are?"

Roger wasn't sure. The only things he knew about demons were from tales, quite frightening ones.

He moved his back away from the tree. A slight pain made him remember.

He then laid himself on the ground, using his arm as a pillow.

"Oh, and if you're hungry, please endure it and leave the horse alive," he mumbled, half asleep.

"Ha?! What do you think demons..."

Her voice quickly drifted away into the distance while Roger hurried to the land of dreams.

Chapter 2

Roger found himself collapsed on the ground. It was night, only darkness around him.

Slowly he rose, supporting himself on the nearby wall. Where was he?

He took a few steps. His legs felt heavy. They didn't move like he wanted.

He noticed sounds coming from all directions. People were screaming. Quick footsteps hit the ground. He could hear their lost hope, their despair.

He looked up towards the sky. Before him an intense, red glow illuminated the sky.

He began walking closer. His legs carried him through the alleys. He turned left around the corner, his feet still unsteady. Then heard a familiar sound. It was the crackling of flames.

He walked another few steps to the next corner. Then he turned right.

The sight in front of him blinded his eyes. A mother with a child in her arms was running away, an older couple struggling to leave the place in a hurry, men a similar age raced from the danger.

Roger stared at the flames. They had engulfed a building, tall like a tower. Everything around it was shrouded in darkness.

Unconsciously he took a few steps closer. He couldn't avert his eyes.

Then he heard his name. Someone was calling him.

He turned his head towards the voice and saw her. Lili was standing in the distance. She was crying, yet smiling.

His legs moved on their own. He started running towards her, his hand stretching out, trying to grasp her. She just stood there watching him.

He was drawing closer, but yet she moved further away. Her figure became smaller and smaller until she had disappeared.

A loud crackling of the flames next to him drew his attention. He realized that he stood on the same spot as before.

Then he saw someone emerging from the flames. Her red eyes made her unmistakable. It was Lili again, walking towards him, but in her demon form.

Then it occurred to him. Was it her? Was it her that caused this?

Then the girl suddenly disappeared again. The ground was shaking. His vision went up and down. He felt something on his left shoulder. It was as if someone was shaking him.

Eventually, his vision went black.

"Hey! Wake up!" he heard in the distance.

"It's already bright!"

The voice was closer this time. He slowly opened his eyes.

He was blinded by the sudden change in brightness. Slowly he could make out trees, grass and various other plants that reflected the soft shine of the morning sun. He saw the logs of the campfire that had turned to ash.

Then a face moved in front of him.

"I'm hungry!" she declared.

Then Roger realized what had happened. It was a dream, just a dream.

He slowly pushed himself off the ground, his body still heavy from the night.

"I'm hungry, I said!"

He looked at her and remembered the dream. Would she do something like that?

His body was slowly waking up until his eyes assumed their usual size. He now saw her face more clearly. Was she pouting? A demon? She looked just like any human girl. Perhaps even a bit more childish.

"Did you hear me?"

"Oh, yes, I did… you said you were hu—"

Roger stopped his words and turned his head hastily.

He saw the horse standing where he had left it yesterday. He made a huge sigh.

"It's still there…"

"Ha?! How rude! What do you think demons are? Beasts?" she shouted, throwing him an angry look.

He looked at her, uncomfortably putting up a forced smile, but for some reason his acting skills weren't as usual. His smile fell apart on one side.

Then Lili came closer, too close.

Her face neared his own just like last night at the church. Roger instinctively pulled his head back.

He tried escaping her by crawling backwards but was quickly stopped by the harsh bark of the familiar tree.

He searched for an escape from her big eyes but to no avail. But they weren't red as before, just very dark.

"I'm sorry… then… what do you want to eat?" Roger asked, trying to calm her down.

She pulled her face back and assumed a standing pose, facing to his left. Her mantle opened at the front and he could see her crossed arms. She made it clear that his words had offended her.

Roger turned to his bag and pulled out a loaf of bread.

"I only have this with me…"

She moved her head slightly and took a doubtful glance at the bread. She didn't move for a few moments until she lashed out at him.

When Roger realized what happened, he saw her eating—no, devouring the bread like a glutton. He squeezed his fingers together confirming that it was indeed the loaf he had in his hands moments ago.

Roger rose, brushing the dirt off his pants. He then observed her as she ate.

"Don't you know the word restraint?" he commented on her unsightly behavior.

She stopped her infesting for a moment and threw Roger a hostile look.

"Leave me alone! I didn't eat anything for over a thousand years!" she said before continuing with her meal.

Roger's hand met his forehead as he let out a huge sigh. How did he get himself in this situation? This was all because he became a Seeker. In addition to hiding his identity from the world, he now had a demon queen at his side, eating up his provisions at fleeting speeds.

He bowed down to pick up his bag and pulled out the last loaf.

He took a bite. A short sensation of pain occurred the moment his teeth hit the crust. He remembered. Because of his sudden escape, he didn't get to buy more food. All he had left were those two loafs. One of which was already gone and the other had the consistency of a brick. But he didn't have anything else.

His face tensed up as his teeth fought the battle against the bread.

Then he noticed Lili glancing at him. She had a smug look and covered her obvious smile with her flat hand. She once again had shown the difference in strength between her race and humans.

Roger chose to ignore her and walked to the horse. He was binding his bag to the saddle when he asked, "So, what are you going to do?"

"I'll have you buy me some clothes!"

He stopped binding for a moment and then continued. Even without looking he could hear her teasing smile. This demon wanted to freeload.

"Just because you're a demon queen, doesn't mean you get everything you desire," he stated coldly as he finished binding and turned around.

"Then, perhaps, you want me to go back to the church and talk to the priest?"

Roger's mouth opened, but he couldn't find the words. She had the upper hand. He couldn't have her running around freely. Perhaps much further away they could part but certainly not so close to Spirithelm.

"It would be a problem for me if you just ran off," he admitted, averting his gaze.

Then she suddenly came closer pushing her face into his again.

"Then you'll buy me clothes?"

He realized there was nothing he could do. As long as she accompanied him, he needed to provide her with the basic necessities or she would stand out. And unwanted suspicion was the least he needed in this situation.

"I'll buy you some," he stated reluctantly, turning his head away. Roger escaped her stare and grabbed the rein. "We're leaving! Jump on the horse."

Roger turned around to help her up, but the moment she entered his vision, she was already in the air and landed on the horse's back that raised its voice in protest. Her eyes had flashed red for a moment.

"When I said jump, I didn't mean that literally."

"How should I know what humans mean with their words? If you say jump, I'll jump!" she called down from the horse.

"Are you a dog or something?"

"Ha? A dog? Your words one day might bring trouble upon you! Of course, I'll only do what I want," she declared royally.

"Sure, sure."

Roger climbed the horse and took the rein in both hands.

"That was one *sure* too much," she told him from

behind.

Roger now realized how small she really was compared to him. Her voice came from a fair way below his neck. When she stood, she seemed taller. Perhaps her royalty made her appear that way, he thought.

"Sure," he corrected, setting the horse into motion. "If you don't hold onto me, you'll fall off."

"Oh?" she said teasingly. "Are you sure you want a demon hold onto you?"

"You can, of course, do want you want. Just don't complain after—"

"Ah!"

Roger was interrupted by a shriek.

The forest ground had given in where the horse stepped, causing Lili to almost fall off.

"I'll take up on your offer then," she proclaimed, defeated, putting her hands around his waist.

Roger let out a chuckle.

"What's so funny?" Lili lashed out.

"No, nothing," he said, maneuvering around a tree. "But I'll appreciate it if you don't bite or anything."

"Are you mocking me perhaps?"

Roger had to smile.

"You're imagining things! I just want to be careful with demons," he told her half-seriously.

She delayed her answer for a moment.

"By asking them not to bite?"

"Well, there are many tales about demons…"

"Tales? Ha! Ha-ha-ha!" she said, bemused. "I wish to hear them one day!"

She pulled on his waist as she leaned backwards to give her laughter way.

"Perhaps, I'll tell you one in the coming days. But you'll be disappointed. They are far from the truth."

"Really? How so?"

"Well… in the tales, demons are bloodthirsty, evil manslayers!"

They were indeed scary tales, but they were just tales after all. If they were true, he would have lost his life the moment he saw her red eyes in the church.

"That sounds truthful, no?"

A shiver ran down Roger's back for a moment.

She was just teasing him, he told himself.

"A-at least the demons I know don't seem like the tales…"

"You know of other demons?" she asked, confused.

"No…" he admitted, giving way to a moment of silence.

He felt fingers burying themselves deeper into his waist.

"Should I show you then? The true nature of demons?" she whispered closely into his ear, her voice too sweet to be taken seriously.

"Please not. Otherwise, I can't buy you clothes."

"Then after that, perhaps?"

Roger remained silent for a while.

"I was joking. Don't fear! Or no, do fear! Humans are supposed to fear demons!"

He had a feeling she was right, but his fear of her had vanished when she collapsed inside the church. Thinking of the pursuit of a hundred knights would cause him to break a cold sweat likelier.

"Perhaps another time. The situation is binding me, sadly enough."

They reached the end of the forest, just a few quick steps away from the main road.

Roger looked in both directions. Luckily he couldn't see anyone and that meant no knights that were coming for them.

"Not that I know of it, but where are we heading?" Lili asked after they entered the main road.

"The city up ahead is called Prok. It's a small city but has a market with a range of goods."

"Like clothes?"

He felt her arms around his waist pulling tighter. She seemed to be very keen on human clothes, even though she was a demon.

"Of course they have clothes, but…" he began, pausing for a moment.

"But?"

"I assume it'll take us more than a day to arrive there."

"I've slept for a thousand years. Certainly, I can endure a day of travel."

"That's not the issue, or I'm glad it isn't. I'm always traveling after all. I'm talking about food. The two loafs of bread were the last ones."

"Ha?! Are you telling me to starve?!"

"I'm sorry I didn't get to buy anything. I was busy carrying the demon queen in person out of town!"

There was a moment of silence.

"You carried me?" she then said insecurely.

"Did you think I teleported you in the forest?"

He felt her hands losing some of their strength.

"I sure have fallen from grace," she lamented.

There was nothing Roger could say against it. She was

a demon queen, but her race was long gone.

Both of them didn't say anything for a while.

Then Roger chose to speak up. Even if the topic wasn't joyful, it would still serve its purpose as a distraction for her.

"So, about the food…" he continued.

"Hm?"

"There are only dry plains ahead. I'm afraid there's nothing to hunt or gather…"

"So, you're really planning on letting me starve? Didn't your tales tell you anything about starving demons?" she asked, tightening her grip from behind.

"Sure, they did. But again, think about the clothes."

"I'm sure yours will do!"

Roger sincerely wished she wouldn't joke around like that. He was almost sure she was truly joking, but his body wasn't so easily convinced.

"I won't give them to you without blood stains."

"Well, perhaps you leave me no choice. But I expect a large feast when we arrive," she declared royally.

"Then we share a common goal for now."

They had traveled quite a bit when Roger noticed a few strands of her black hair swinging back and forth in rhythm with the horse.

"Isn't your hair inconvenient when it's so long?"

"No," she declared. "I like my hair."

"Just wondering, but did your hair grow over the thousand years?"

"They are just like I remember them. If they had grown over the years, I wouldn't need any clothes now."

"Truly," he answered, imagining her body entangled in way too long hair.

He saw her hair vanish behind him and felt her pulling on his waist. He turned his head.

He saw her bending backwards over at her waist, looking at the sky behind.

She was an odd girl, he thought.

He decided to leave her be and turned back to the front.

Roger looked in the far distance. There was nothing other than a road and dry grass to their sides.

That was all they saw for the next day and half until they could make out the borders of the promised city ahead.

It was surrounded by stone walls to keep unwanted folk out. The only way in was following the road and entering through the gate at the end. That involved convincing the guards that one was an admirable person that ought to be entering the city.

Luckily, Roger had been to many cities, just not with company and certainly not with a demon.

"Lili, pull your hood up and hide your face and..." Roger began, pausing for a moment.

"And?"

"...can you please do something about your hair? It will only raise suspicion," he asked carefully.

To his surprise she seemed to understand his intentions and said, "I see. It can't be helped..."

Roger saw the strands being pulled up bit by bit.

"Just make sure it doesn't show while we're passing the guards. When we're in the city, we'll walk."

Conveniently, the mantle he had lent her reached almost to the ground when she was standing up straight. It was perfect to hide her hair.

Roger rode closer to the guards and eventually stopped right before them.

One guard walked to their side and looked at Roger.

"Sir, your reason of stay," he asked with a voice full of boredom.

The guard was asking purely out of routine. He had no personal interest. However, those kind of guards were particularly frightening for Roger. At a first glance they appeared to be willing to let through anyone because they weren't interested in their job. But that was not the case. They were bored. They were desperately trying to find opportunities to escape their boredom. If they noticed anything off on one of the travelers trying to enter, their eyes would double in size.

"We've come to visit the church," Roger answered with a perfect smile. Of course, it was entirely a farce. Roger took no joy in fooling guards.

"Oh? The church you say?" the guard commented, raising an eyebrow. He turned his eyes towards Lili clinging onto Rogers back, burying her face into it.

Roger intentionally chose this situation since Lili could easily pass as a nun. He didn't want to take the risk of the guard finding something strange about her. And since the guards had to be very careful if their job involved people from the church, his story was perfect.

The guard turned his head back to Roger.

"Your wife, perhaps?"

"I'm glad you can tell!" Roger answered, keeping up his smile. "She's not used to long travels and is a bit tired."

"Naturally," the guard agreed. "Where did you come from?"

"From the south, a small village named Shimmerspire."

Roger did indeed come from the south at some point, but Spirithelm was more to the east. There was no need to raise suspicion by saying they came from that direction.

"Ah! Shimmerspire. I've heard of it. Has a fine church, people say."

Roger could tell that it was a lie. The guard's eyes avoided his before he started speaking.

It was not a bad strategy. People from the church believed in the goodwill of people and most likely wouldn't notice. And getting on the church's good side was a good choice of the guard. Perhaps word would spread of his good manners and he got a promotion. It was entirely possible that the word of church people could change this guard's fate, for better or for worse.

"I'm glad our humble church is viewed in such lights."

The guard just put up a quick smile in response. His eyes wandered over the horse and stopped at Roger's bag. Surely he wouldn't ask to have a look inside. He would enter dangerous territory if they were really from the church.

"May I ask you what you're carrying?" the guard asked without hesitation.

Roger felt that something was odd. Normally, the guard would just let them pass if he saw that they were from the church, but it seemed like he was still suspicious.

Roger turned his head towards his bag, taking a glimpse of Lili.

Her face wasn't visible and she looked like she was sleeping. He looked further down but didn't catch any strands hanging down. There was no doubt that she could pass as a nun.

He turned towards the guard and smiled. "We're carrying a sacred relic and were asked to deliver it to Prok's church," he said, opening his bag slightly and pulling out the fire steel.

He held it in both hands to make the impression that it was actually valuable. It had burn marks of various color tones on it, making it indeed look like it could have been from the distant past.

Roger held it low enough for the guard to see but far enough so that the guard didn't get the impression that he could inspect it. To him it was a sacred relic after all. It would be impious if he were to even ask whether he could touch it.

"Oh, such honor. I've never seen a sacred relic up close. It indeed looks like it has been through times, very impressive!"

He was fooled, but that was to be expected. Guards didn't have a particularly high social stand. They wouldn't be knowledgeable on sacred relics.

"Due to the heat we were forced to make quite a few breaks and we're already late. I'd like to deliver it as early as possible," Roger pressed the guard to avoid getting any more questions or reasons to raise suspicion.

"Oh, my apologies. It's just always a pleasure to meet people from the church. You may pass," he flattered, bowing his head slightly.

Roger set his horse into motion.

"God's blessings on you!"

He turned to the front and passed the gate.

Roger and Lili had successfully entered the city without any incidents.

They rode along the main street. It was wide enough for ten people to stand side by side.

After a while, Roger could feel Lili pulling her face away from his back. He felt her stretching up his back and then her gentle breath on his left ear. A weird shiver ran down his body.

"You're three hundred years too early to claim me your wife!" she whispered with a teasing tone in her voice.

Roger was taken aback for a moment, but quickly gathered himself again and spoke up.

"It was the most rational option to go with the guard's fantasies. It gives him some gratification that he was right, making him easier to convince."

He looked around at the few citizen on their way, making sure nobody listened in on their conversation. It were mostly mothers with their children doing the work of housewives.

"You're quite the rational one. Are all Seekers like this?"

"I assume they are. I've never met another, or perhaps I just didn't notice. But a Seeker will go to great lengths to decipher a spell if they wish for it or not."

"I see. But I've to say you're quite good at fooling your fellow humans. Ah-ha-ha-ha!"

She laughed into his back, her voice getting muffled

by his coat.

"If I wasn't, I wouldn't have come this far. I would be rotting in the ground by now."

Then he remembered some of her words from earlier.

"Did you say three hundred years?"

"Huh?" She raised her face from his coat. "I did indeed."

"How old are you exactly?"

Suddenly, Roger felt two stinging pains on his sides.

"How rude! Even demons are conscious about their age," she said, perhaps pouting.

"But you did say three hundred..."

"I did."

Roger thought to himself for a moment. He didn't know how old demons got typically. Before she appeared, it was an average of exactly zero years. But since she had said three hundred years, did that mean she was over three hundred years old? A girl as small as her? Even though she could be mistaken for a twelve year-old human girl?

She looked young indeed, but he could tell that she wasn't twelve. She was demon queen of her race and her way of acting wasn't fit for a twelve year-old, or so he thought...

"Hey! What's this?! Those shiny colored things?" she called out, raising her voice way too loud while leaning into the direction of a fruit stand they just passed.

She had almost pulled him off the horse in the process.

He gently pressed his legs against the horse and tightened his grip on the rein. The horse came to a halt and he turned around to look closer at the stand.

"Those are apples. You've never seen those?"

"Apples? What a fine name! No, we mostly eat monster parts," she revealed casually.

Even though she had such a small body, after what happened to the loaf of bread he gave her, he could easily imagine her eating, or rather devouring some monsters.

Roger heard a growling sound coming from behind.

"You promised me a feast, remember?" she muttered shyly, trying to cover up her stomach tumults.

"I sure did. But first we have to buy some clothes for you."

"But we can't exactly do that on an empty stomach, can we? Imagine what would happen if I were to collapse in the middle of a crowd."

Roger heard it in her voice that she thought she had the upper hand in this discussion. Sadly enough she really did.

"Don't even try that. There's no telling what would happen."

"Then in contributions to preventing that, perhaps some apples would help."

Roger let out a sigh. He was hungry himself, but it wasn't that he couldn't wait until after. There were times were he had to get by without food for far more than one day.

"Stay on the horse, I'll buy you some," he said reluctantly, stepping down to the street.

He walked to the fruit stand. An old woman was standing behind it and smiled at him.

"I'll take three apples."

"Three apples coming up," she said in a soft voice fit for her age.

She took a thin piece of fabric and put one apple after the other on it. After the third, she put another one on top and wrapped the fabric skillfully into a package.

"Excuse me, I wanted three, not four."

"It's three and one as a present. Your wife seems really eager to eat them." She looked behind Roger as she spoke.

He turned around. Lili was staring at the package with wide eyes, almost drooling. Roger turned back to the fruit woman.

"It's two silver coins," she said with a smile.

Roger pulled out two pieces from his purse attached to his pants and handed them to the woman.

"Sure. Thank you for your kindness." He gave her a smile back.

She took the two silver pieces and gave him the apples.

"Since your wife was so looking forward to the apples, I just had to."

Roger expressed his thanks again and walked back to the horse. He handed Lili the apples and mounted. They continued their way into the city.

Roger could hear munching sounds from behind.

"Um, delicious," she approved happily, shoving the next apple into her mouth. "Um~"

Even if she looked like a human girl without her demon attributes, she certainly didn't behave like a human queen.

Roger didn't need to turn around to know that it wouldn't take long before all the apples were gone. But perhaps any human queen would have behaved the same if they had been sealed for a thousand years.

Roger put that thought aside and continued following the street.

The number of people was increasing steadily. At one point it became so crowded they would have been faster without the horse. But Roger's intention had been from the start to sell it and continue by foot. There wasn't really a need for a horse in a city, unless it was a really big one. He had great respect for the horse to show so much enduring. But soon it'd be someone else's.

After a while Roger finally had managed to reach one of the stables in the city. It was a place were one could sell and buy horses, a blessing for any traveler.

Roger slowly entered the stables with the horse and scanned its insides. He saw three horses waiting patiently for their new owner, but Roger was more interested in the whereabouts of their current. He turned his head left and right several times, but all he saw were the horses.

Then he felt Lili pulling on his fabric from behind. He turned his head and spotted Lili's hand, pointing towards the back corner of the stable.

Roger carefully navigated the horse further in to see what was lurking there. As Roger passed the horse blocking his sight, he had found the owner; however, not in a state he had liked to find him.

On the ground before him, a man was spread out, his head supported by the muddy wall. He had an open skin lying on one of his hands and a belly that raised no questions about the skin's contents. His eyes were closed, quite in contrast to his mouth that was hanging to his collarbones. But he wasn't dead. His round belly was moving up and down accompanied by an occasional grunt.

"What do we have here?" Lili asked, regarding the man from behind.

"Hopefully a stray citizen drowning in the pleasures of city live and not the stable owner," Roger said, not doubting at any point in time that this man was indeed the stable owner.

"What are you going to do? You wanted to sell the horse, no?"

Roger stepped down from the horse and walked up to the man. He crouched down next to his face and shook him on the shoulder.

"Excuse me, Sir! Sir!" he said repeatedly as he made his voice gradually become louder.

Then after several attempts, the man opened his eyes slowly after several loud grunts. He mindlessly glanced off into space until Roger raised his voice again.

"Sir, I'm here to sell my horse."

The drunken man finally turned his head, although very slowly. Roger could tell that the man's mind was anything but there.

"Are you the stable owner, perhaps?"

The man turned his head back to his front and awkwardly tried getting up, spilling the rest contents of the skin that had fallen out of his hand.

He pushed himself against the wall in an attempt to get up. Roger decided to help him out and after a few moments the man stood, not very steadily, but at least standing. He placed his hand on the wall to support his balance.

"I'd like to sell my horse," Roger reminded him.

The man looked at him and then at the horse to his front. He raised his head slowly until he stopped at the mighty Lili sitting on its back.

"I've come here with it from Ashana, a small territory in the east."

"A-A-Ashwana??" the man stumbled.

"That's correct. Of course, it has fortified steel horseshoes." He pointed at the horseshoes that were dyed in a rusty red.

"Ohh…" the man let out a breathy affirmation.

"It has very good stamina and traveled the whole way without additional rest."

"Ohh," he breathed again.

Beside his grunts from earlier this sound seemed to be the most the man was capable in this state, Roger concluded.

"I bought it for three gold pieces, but since it's come a long way let's make it just two," Roger offered in his best bargain voice.

"Two… gold…" The man's eyes widened slowly while he panted out his words.

"It is a horse you'll only encounter once in your life," Roger said, smiling at him.

The man didn't say anything for a few moments.

"What do you say?" Roger pressed.

The man took a heavy breath and turned his attention to his purse hanging on his belt. He dug through its contents and then finally offered Roger the gold pieces he wanted.

Roger smiled and took the coin.

"It was a pleasure to do business with you," he encountered. "Lili, come down, we'll leave," he said, walking towards the exit.

When he exited the stables, Lili came running after him. Roger continued to walk the street.

"Are you sure you want to sell such a horse?"

"Of course I do. I bought it for fifty silver pieces in a town before Spirithelm," he told her. "That's half a gold piece."

She showed him a perplex expression initially but quickly turned it into a mischievous smile.

"I see. Perhaps you're more of a demon than some real ones."

"Me? A demon? That was his own fault and I have to get my money from somewhere. I can't just work somewhere, you know?"

"Ha-ha-ha! I'm not objecting, just an observation. I think I'm starting to get what kind of man you are," she said laughingly.

What did she mean by that? Surely there was no one in this world that could understand him unless they were a Seeker themselves. But Seeker's did not share paths and if they were to meet, they most likely wouldn't notice. The thought that a demon was the only one who understood him was preposterous.

"Save your remarks for later and look to the front," Roger said while pointing at the marketplace ahead.

As the street opened into a wide plaza, the number of people seemed to decrease, although it was the opposite. But now they had enough space to comfortably look through the different stands.

They continued walking further in while Lili gazed at the vast variety of goods being sold there with sparkly eyes.

It was a marketplace living up to its reputation. Quite different than the one in Spirithelm. Here, one could obtain anything from food to armor and weapons, decorations to potions, and most importantly clothes, the primary reason why Roger had come to this place.

Lili was still wearing just a black mantle with nothing underneath. The mantle helped conceal both her wings and tail but its practicality had its limits. And perhaps they would find something that helped with her hair. Roger had refrained from suggesting to cut it. He wasn't sure if he would have lived through that. But at least he could buy something she could use to tie it up.

Roger had arrived at the clothing stands he was searching for. A large variety of clothes with different colors and purposes was laid out before them. He stopped before one of the stands and turned to Lili. It was hard to miss the excitement in her face. Perhaps girls from all races were interested in clothes, even demons.

Roger bowed down and whispered in her ear.

"We need one set of clothes to hide your wings and tail, and you can pick another one for when we're not among people," he said generously. After all, he had just obtained enough money to comfortably afford it.

She turned her head and looked at him like a child having her dearest wish granted.

"I'll look around to buy some other things. Just be careful."

"Sure!" she encountered happily.

She gave off the impression of being just a carefree human girl. But he was sure she was aware of her situation. She was the queen of the demon race after all, even if she was the last one remaining.

Roger took a step back and turned around. He continued looking through the market. The first thing he needed was another mantle. If things came to worse and they were to be discovered, a black mantle for each of them would be vital to hide in the darkness of the night.

After a while of walking around the clothing area, he found one that sold those. Mantles were originally intended give protection from the harsh weather when traveling, but as a Seeker he needed to use them in different ways to get by.

He simply picked one of the mantles before him and paid for it. There was no need to waste time finding the right one. In the end, it was just a plain mantle.

The next thing he needed was some food for the travels up ahead. He had memorized the maps of Alurona and knew that none of the adjacent cities were particularly close. And only one and a half days had passed since he had conducted the ritual. Until three days had passed, he wouldn't know which direction he needed to go next, so he had to cover all the possibilities.

He headed a bit further to reach the area where they sold food. As a traveler it was essential that he picked food that quickly sated. He didn't have the luxury to carry around an abundance of food. Everything needed to fit in the bag he had with him at all times. It was possible to obtain food in the wild by hunting monsters or gathering plants, but especially close to the cities, most area was used for growing crops and monsters generally didn't go near human settlements. So if he couldn't obtain food in the wild, he needed to bring it with him. Luckily, most cities and towns were at most two days of traveling apart. It was unlikely that he needed more than that.

But of course, now that he somehow ended up bringing a demon girl along, he had to carry double the amount. Lili didn't complain about the loaf of bread she ate, so he decided to buy another few. If eaten within a few days, they were still comfortably chewable and tasted reasonably well. The only issue he had with the bread was the occasional pebbles that made their way into the dough. But still they were a good choice, even at the cost of a few teeth.

He still had the three skins of silver oil he had bought in Spirithelm. There was no need to buy any more of those. The only thing missing was something that helped with Lili's hair. It wasn't an exaggeration to say it was uncommon to see hair of such length. Most girls her age didn't have to do much with their hair besides a bit of brushing to keep the dirt away. Girls of nobility usually had some spruce worked into it and perhaps a braided tail or two, but that didn't help the length of her hair nor did it help his purse. The best he could think of was a sturdy piece of cloth that could be used to bind her hair up. If they went into a tavern a bit later in the day, he couldn't possibly let her cover the floor with her hair.

Roger walked around looking for stands that sold things related to hair. The stands in questions usually weren't particularly hard to find. A crowd of young women gathering in one place was a good indicator.

As he approached the suspected stands, he could see the glistening jewels sparkling at him from a distance. When he arrived behind the crowd, he looked for stands that sold hair accessories. Since he was about a head taller than most women there, he didn't need to fight his way through the crowds.

After checking out a few stands, he finally found one that sold hair related goods.

"Oh, what an unusual guest. You looking for a present?" the middle-aged woman behind the stand greeted him friendlily.

"I guess I am. I'm looking for something that can be used to tie up very long hair," he answered with a smile.

"Long hair, you say? Are we talking about hip-long hair, perhaps?"

"Unfortunately, it's more the length of knee-long..." he admitted, scratching the back of his head.

She covered her mouth with both of her hands in admiration.

"Oh my! She must be such a beauty with hair this long!"

"I guess she is," he answered, abashed. Of course, this was only on the surface. He had actually never thought about her beauty before. Was it even possible to measure up the human understanding of beauty against a demon? He was sure the woman in front of him would have a better answer to that question, but he decided to refrain asking.

"Then how about this one?" She presented him with a white ribbon. "It's the thickest I have for sale. I'm sure you could tie up hair twice as long as hers, but that would be a bit much for the girl! Ha-ha!" She laughed warmly.

Roger laughed back, although he was sure that she could carry even ten times the weight on her head.

He looked at the ribbon in question. He couldn't

picture her wearing white in her hair. That wouldn't fit and he didn't want to buy it only to hear her complains afterward. He remembered when he first met her. If she had any color associated with her, it would be the red in her eyes. Her hair, wings and tail were all black.

"Do you have it in red?"

"Let me see…"

She took a step back and looked below her stand. Then she pulled two additional ribbons in red from below. "Those are the only two. I don't often have people buy these," she said in a slightly apologetic voice.

"I guess that makes sense, but two are more than enough. I'll take them."

"Surely! That will be one silver coin."

Roger pulled out one silver coin from his purse and handed it to her. She took it and put the two ribbons in its place.

"It was a plea—"

She stopped her own words and took another item from her stand. "One of these would make a nice addition, I think… what do you say?"

She presented Roger with a hair brush.

"What do I say? I'm not sure…"

Roger didn't have much experience with girls. All he had were memories from his childhood, but back then the girls didn't care about their hair that much.

"If the hair's as long as you say, it must be quite troublesome keeping it clean. I think this would be perfect!" she said happily.

To Roger everything the woman said made sense. But she could tell him a lot about women's hair and he wouldn't be able to tell truth from lie. But her words sounded very convincing. He hadn't taken a closer look at Lili's hair before, but it probably had picked up a lot of dirt from their travels.

"Then I'll take it in addition."

"Wonderful. That would be two silver pieces."

Roger paid for the brush and put it in his bag together with the ribbons.

"It was a pleasure doing business with you," he told her, smiling.

She returned the gesture and he then headed back to where Lili was.

She was standing in front of one of the stands and waited. She noticed him while he was still a handful of stands away.

Then she showed him all the pieces she had picked, and Roger proceeded buying them.

"Are these all?" Roger asked her.

"They are indeed."

Roger could tell she was in a good mood, but she didn't have the same childishness in her voice as earlier.

"How much are these?" he asked the stand owner, a muscular middle-aged man standing behind a sea of clothes with his arms crossed.

"Pants, coat, a dress and shoes... that'll be 84 silver pieces," he answered plainly.

Roger didn't think it would be this much, but together with his other expenses today, including the inn for the night, he still had made a sizable profit from his horse deal earlier. Roger paid the man without complaint and exchanged the usual phrase.

The sun was already on its way down and the sooner

the better they needed to find an inn to stay the night. It didn't take them long before they reached one. Most service buildings targeted towards travelers were located close to the market. Having a store close to the walls would only bring in locals as customers, not profitable enough for most stores to survive.

Roger and Lili entered the inn and he payed for a room for the night.

Like the inn in Spirithelm the rooms were on the upper floor and a tavern on the ground level.

Both went upstairs and entered their new room. Roger closed the door behind them.

It had a double bed in the middle and a small table at the wall. Again, Lili was mistaken as his wife and he was given a room for a couple instead of one with two separate beds. It seemed like traveling with a female was impossible in this world without her being one's wife.

He walked across the room to the only window and opened the covers. Then he leaned outside putting his arms on the frame as support.

There was a row of market stands on the other side of the street. Those stand owners didn't make it onto the main marketplace, so they had to settle for a street leading to it. The city charged a fee to grant a stand license. The closer the stands were to the main marketplace, the higher the charges. And additionally, the sellers needed to part with a percentage of their hard earned money to the city. It was the cruel world of trading. If he could exchange his life as a Seeker for the one of a trader, he would think twice. At least he got to see the world and wasn't chained to his stand and the caprice of the viscount.

Roger realized he had been lost in thought for a while. He wondered what Lili was up to since she had remained quiet the whole time.

He turned around and looked at her. As quickly as he turned, he reversed his motion and continued looking, or rather staring outside the window.

Lili was standing in front of the bed, naked, her new clothes neatly spread out on the bed. She seemed to have trouble deciding.

"Keep in mind we need to go downstairs to eat."

"Surely I can tell that. It's just that I haven't worn clothes made by humans before," she said in admiration.

That made Roger think. What kind of clothes did demons wear when they were still alive? Or did they even have clothes in the first place? The demon girl behind him sometimes made the impression they had not.

"How were the clothes back then?"

She took a few moments to respond.

"Hm… if I compare them to those, they didn't have as much fabric. And of course, there were holes for wings and tail."

Roger imagined how they would look like. He thought the dress she had picked was considered low on fabric. If it was winter, she'd turn to ice wearing that.

His gaze wandered around the people walking down on the street. They were covered in fabric and it was the climax of summer.

"Isn't that cold?" he asked her. "What clothes did you wear in winter?"

"Winter? What is that?" she asked, confused.

His eyes stopped for a moment. She didn't know

winter? The chilliest season filled with dangerous snow storms and cold trying to take away a man's every limp?

Winter was without a doubt the harshest season for Seekers. Only suicidal travelers would attempt to continue from one place to another. But Seekers didn't have the luxury of taking shelter in a city. They were driven towards their next ancient spell. There was no escaping it.

For a while, Roger was reliving some memories of the five winters he had lived through as a Seeker. He wondered how the winter this year would turn out.

"Hey! What is winter, I say," Lili protested.

"Oh, I'm sorry. I was just..." he answered as she brought him back to his senses. "Winter is the name for one of the four seasons in Alurona. It's a very cold season where the lands turn white."

If Lili didn't know winter, did that mean that back then in the demon realm, they didn't have the four seasons?

"The lands turn white?" she said excitedly. "I'd surely like to see that one day."

That confirmed his theory.

"In the demon realm... how's the weather there?"

There wasn't much tell about the demon realm. The only thing he had heard about it was its name, Valzeraresh, that it was once called. But no map showed its location nor did he meet anyone that claimed having been there before. If demons no longer lived there, what happened to the realm now?

"I'm not sure how it is now, but in comparison to here, it was considerably higher in temperature. I've heard that the weather changes here, but we don't have anything like that. It's always the same."

It being hotter explained the clothes at least, but the demon realm was still far beyond Roger's comprehension. It didn't seem anything like Alurona, the only realm he ever saw. Everything he knew about other realms, he had heard from somewhere.

"Can we eat now?"

He turned around and looked at the luckily now dressed Lili. Her brown pants were surrounded by her black hair, and at the top it was a light summery coat. There wasn't any sign of her demon attributes.

"Can you turn around for a bit?" he asked.

Her smile turned pleased and she swung around elegantly on one leg.

The coat had a hood attached at the back. It was covering parts of where her wings should have been, but he couldn't make them out. But that was because they were rather small. So small, it raised the question if she could actually fly with those. But nonetheless, Roger was impressed how well the coat hid them.

Looking further down, he made a similar observation. Her tail was nowhere to be seen. He wondered where it went. Maybe she had slung it around her waist, wearing it like a belt. He, of course, had no idea how comfortable or uncomfortable it had to be, having to store a tail as long as hers inside a pair of pants.

But still, even if her demon attributes were dealt with, there was still the matter of her hair. It just stood out. Attention that he certainly wasn't asking for.

He walked over to his bag being closely observed by Lili and pulled out the two red ribbons he bought. He held them in front of her.

"Here. I know you like your hair, but perhaps you can tie them up a bit for as long we eat?"

She looked at the red strings of cloth with big eyes.

"You—you bought them for me?" Her voice was filled with humble surprise. Then she looked at Roger.

He just looked back and didn't say anything.

Then she carefully reached for the ribbons with her two tiny hands and took them carefully. She held them like they were a treasure, even though it were just two pieces of cheap fabric.

She looked at them for some time in admiration and then raised her head again.

"How do you use them?"

Roger couldn't hide a glimpse of surprise in his face.

"Didn't you have something like that back then?"

She shook her head silently.

Roger was in a pinch. He, having last spend time with a girl more than five years ago, was as clueless as the demon in front of him. But he couldn't let this show. Admitting he bought her the ribbons without knowing how to put them to use was out of the question.

"I-if you don't mind, I can show you." His voice had less confidence then he had hoped for.

"You may," she answered plumply, giving him the ribbons. Then she turned around.

He needed to somehow tie them up so that they weren't be visible under her coat. He had exactly two ribbons to accomplish that job.

Her hair seemed far longer than it appeared before. When he stood right behind her, he couldn't even see the end of it.

He took a step back and kneed down on one leg. Then

he carefully collected a bundle of hair at the bottom, making it roughly half of all the hairs she had. Slowly, he lifted them up towards the top. When he reached her neck, he took the ribbon and threaded it through half of the strands at the top. In his final step he bound the bundle of hairs in his hand together with her neck-level hair. He added a loop, thinking it would look nicer on a girl than just two hanging ends.

He looked at her from behind. The length of her hair was now halved. It certainly wasn't praiseworthy, but it did what it should. If she wore the coat above it, nobody would see her unusually long hair. He gave off a satisfied smile and bound the other side, following the same procedure.

And finally, he had fulfilled his task. He didn't need to be taught by a girl. He could bind ribbons just fine. Lili's back now showed two red ribbons with a loop each. Even if Lili wasn't impressed, he certainly was.

"Done. You can turn around now," he said, this time more confidently.

She swung her hair around a few times struggling to see behind her back.

"Say, how does it look?" she asked, eyeing him with expectation.

Roger was at loss for words. How did it look, really? It certainly didn't gave off the impression of a feared demon queen, but if he were to judge her looks by human standards, it wasn't too bad. Rather, if she had been a human girl, she would have made a fine wife. But that surely was the least she wanted to hear.

"Good, I guess?"

She showed him an energetic smile. "I commend you,"

she said. "Even humans are capable of some good things."

Any lingering impression of being a human girl was swept away. She was without a doubt not human, a full-fledged demon so to say.

"Just wear your coat on top of your hair and you'll get your promised feast," he returned, grabbing his bag and walking to the door.

Eventually, the two of them ended up taking place in the tavern below and ordered their food. Lili had ordered cooked, sliced and seasoned meat and a beer to drink while Roger settled for a soup full of greens and potatoes combined with meatballs and also a beer. After some time, their food arrived.

The sun had already set and the tavern started filling up gradually.

"Umm! Delicious, indeed!" Lili said with a full mouth, shoving one slice of meat after another inside.

"See? As I promised you!" Roger encountered, taking another spoon.

"Say, for how many days can I enjoy such a meal?"

Two days had passed since Roger conducted the ritual. In about a day he would know where his next spell was located. That's exactly how long Roger could afford to relax in a great city like this.

"The day after tomorrow is when we leave," he answered plumply.

Lili didn't look his way. She was busy working her way through her slices. "I see," was all she answered.

Roger had expected her to be at least dissatisfied having to part with her meals so soon.

He paused eating for a moment and took a gulp of his

beer. He felt the prickling sensation traveling down his throat. Lili followed him suit and also took a break to drink. But as with the food, she didn't show any restraint. With one smooth motion she emptied her mug and slammed it on the wooden table.

She stared at him. Her eyes had become slimmer and her cheeks had reddened up.

"Could it be you don't fare well with alcohol?" he asked in surprise.

"Ha? Alcohol? What's that?" she asked, swinging her head in a circle.

Roger was genuinely startled at her blunt question. Did demons not have alcohol back then? Maybe that was something that should have occurred to him before. There was no doubt it was definitely getting to her.

"It might as well doesn't matter now..." he replied, letting out a sigh.

She swung the empty mug left and right. "You sure are an odd one."

"I don't want to hear that from you," he said, taking one of the meatballs in his mouth.

Suddenly she stood up. "Ha-ha-ha!" she laughed royally. "That may be true!"

Then she walked around the table and sat herself directly next to him, leaving no gap for air in between.

"What are you doing?" Roger asked when she suddenly leaned her head on his arm.

"I'm resting. Can't you see?" There was not a shred of doubt in her voice.

"Sure I can, but... why on my arm?"

She then suddenly shrugged, letting out a hiccup. "Somehow, I'm feeling hot..."

It was hard to state otherwise after taking a look at her. Her cheeks were bright red and her eyes half closed. Her body sat there collapsed, lacking the energy from earlier. She really didn't fare well with alcohol.

"You still have food left. Are you sure you don't want to eat it?"

After all, it was said that food helped dealing with spirits.

"Indeed... I'm still hungry," she realized, slowly lifting herself up.

She pulled the plate over from the other side of the table, then grabbed the fork and put another slice in her mouth. Roger proceeded to do the same with his meatballs.

"What will you do if you find someone and grow close?" Lili asked out of the blue.

It was a surprisingly serious question. Surely that was the spirits' fault.

"That wouldn't happen. I'm constantly on the move," he replied with a full mouth.

"But if it still happens?"

"I would continue as always and leave them behind," he said, staring inside his mug. "Not that I have much choice."

"Hmm...?"

At that moment the door to the tavern smashed open, accompanied by jocular voices. Entering were three guards still in their light armory, mainly consisting of some chain mail. They took place on a table a bit further away from Roger and Lili.

"A beer I'll have!" the first proclaimed to one of the wenches, followed by the others who ordered the same.

"Man, today was a day. The viscount works us hard enough already and now we have to search the whole city," the second complained.

"You said it! Perhaps the age has caught up to the viscount, ordering to search the city for a Seeker and a demon. Absurdity!" the third continued.

The three of them let out a lengthy laughter.

Roger had stopped eating by now, and Lili had pulled the hood over her head.

"Let's wait until they leave. Walking out of the tavern now would only draw attention," he whispered to Lili.

She nodded subtly.

Both of them continued eating, trying to act as naturally as possible while listening to the guards' conversation.

"I've heard there has been an incident in Spirithelm to the east. The church is in shatters and demon feathers have been found under the debris," the second guard told.

Roger's food suddenly stopped in his throat, his eyes wide open. The feathers! He had forgotten about the feathers! He had made a grave mistake. The news had taken quite an exaggeration, but that didn't matter right now. They needed to leave the city immediately, but the night had arrived and the gates were closed. But they certainly couldn't stay at the inn. If the guards inquired about the guests from the inn owner, they would undoubtably visit their room and if Lili was forced to undress, there would be no way to hide her demon attributes. The conclusion that he was a Seeker would follow shortly after that.

Suddenly, Roger shrieked on the inside after hearing a

hiccup from Lili. He glanced over to her, but what drew his attention were the three stares of the guards. Their conversation had come to a halt.

Cold sweat ran down on his back. But this was not the first time he was in such a dire situation. He had no trouble acting like nothing happened, pretending the guards didn't exist. He continued to take another bite, but his calm outer appearance contrasted the inner tumults that kept his mind racing.

But their situation didn't improve. The third guard stood up and slowly walked over to them. Then he placed his hand on Lili's shoulder from behind.

"May I ask you to reveal your face?" he said without a hint of emotion in his voice.

"Ah, we're from the chu—"

Roger attempted to distract the guard but stopped when Lili stood up on the guard's words.

She pretended to lose balance and fell on the man's chest, keeping her head down so that he couldn't see her face. Roger immediately followed up with her act.

"I'm sorry, Sir. She had a bit too much."

Before the guard could speak up again, Lili continued her act.

"Oh, my! Such a sturdy chest you have!" she lied with some slightly slurred speech. He wasn't sure if it was an act or the spirits caused it, but it was a good plan.

In reality Roger knew there was no way she could tell anything about the state of the man's chest through the thick chain mail, but the guard visibly didn't notice that fact. If anything, he looked quite pleased.

"O-oh, thank you…" was all he could reply.

"How the time has passed!" Roger called out,

standing up in false shock. "We still need to visit the priest," Roger proclaimed loudly, looking at the dark street outside the window.

He took Lili's hand and pulled her away from the guard.

In great steps he neared the exit the fastest he could without further raising the guards' suspicion. If he was quick enough, before the guards caught up with the situation, they would vanish into the dark of the night. Even if the guards suspected them, they didn't know for sure. A quite different situation than if they knew for certain that they were the wanted pair.

The third guard was still standing at the table in a state of delusion and the second guard sat on the bench and just watched. But the first guard had stood up and headed their way.

Roger had already opened the door, but then Lili suddenly stopped. He turned around and saw Lili as she picked up something from the ground.

The first guard had reached them.

"Not so fast!" he said in a stern voice. "Under the orders of the viscount, we need to inspect you before you can take your leave," he stated, sounding almost hostile.

"The priest can be quite harsh if left waiting. If he were to learn that guards had kept him waiting, he surely wouldn't be pleased," Roger argued.

It was a bold move but very effective in keeping low-ranked guards at a distance.

"Even if that were the case, it is under the orders of the viscount. Even the priest has to follow them."

He had crossed a line that would bring forth great misfortune upon him if they truly were from the church, but the reason was evident. No matter how one looked at them, they were a suspicious pair. The guard didn't believe a single word he said.

Lili was standing with her back towards the guard. Her face showed an uncomfortable expression and it also showed the effects of the spirits. She looked very tired.

He took her hand again and said his final words to the guard.

"The viscount surely respects the church. If he was here, he'd surely make the right decision. The priest is waiting," Roger said in a hurry. Then he took off and moved outside the tavern leading Lili by her hand.

"What is this?!" the guard shouted from behind.

Roger turned around.

The guard looked down at Lili with widened eyes.

Roger quickly turned his head, looking at Lili in fearing premonition. He saw her holding one of the red ribbons in her hand. When he saw her back, it confirmed his fears. Half of Lili's black hair had fallen beneath her coat, revealing its full length. Somehow that night, her hair looked inhuman. It seemed to swallow up all the light around it, just like the night he first met her.

He clenched his teeth together in anger at himself. He couldn't do it after all. The ribbon he tied didn't hold.

The guard suddenly came charging at the two. Roger was too slow to react and the guard ripped the hood from Lili's head. A scary expression formed in Lili's face and she turned around. Upon meeting Lili's gaze, the guard tumbled back a few steps in fear.

"Oh great lord, it is true..." the guard uttered. "It's them," he shouted to the other guards inside.

They immediately came running. Roger started

running as well, dragging Lili on her hand.

He entered a side alley and kept running with all of his might, but he could feel Lili pulling him back. When he looked back, he saw her panting heavily and her eyes barely stayed open. If he didn't let her order alcohol, if he would have tied the ribbon properly, if he didn't forget her feathers at the church, all of this would have never happened.

The guards had entered the side alley as well. They kept chasing them with great speed and they were getting closer. Roger turned at the next corner and then pulled Lili to his front. He picked her up, carrying her the same as when he escaped the church.

He kept running. The guards had to carry the full weight of their armory. Lili was light in comparison and his physique had helped him out several times in the past, and he believed this would be one of those times.

He kept running, looking back every now and then after some while, he couldn't see the guards anymore. But he still kept running until he arrived at the city's church.

He sat down Lili and leaned her upper body against the church wall. He took out his skeleton keys and made his way with the lock.

"The church…?" Lili said, still panting. "Didn't you tell them… that you wanted to go there?" Her voice sounded brittle.

"That's exactly why it has to be the church. They know who we are. They know we're not from the church. That's why the last place they will search is here."

Lili didn't answer and Roger didn't look at her. He concentrated on picking the lock and then he finally had success and opened the door. He turned towards Lili in an attempt to help her up, but she already was standing on her own. Unsteadily she walked to Roger and then both of them entered the church.

They made their way to the front and sunk down, leaning against the altar. The faint moonlight shone through the tessellated glass panels that reached to the top of the church.

"Pathetic..." Lili spoke up, almost sobbing. "Me a demon queen? Ha! I'm so lacking I can't even fool some lowly humans..."

"No wonder my race is no more..." she added in a faint voice, almost too quiet to hear.

A moment of silence fused with the quiet night.

It was his mistakes that brought this upon them. Roger gazed at the cold stone ground in front of him. A question entered his mind that he wanted to ask since that one night.

He looked at her.

She had pulled her knees close. The soft moonlight shone on her, but both wings and hair stayed pitch black.

"Can I ask you why you were sealed?"

Her expression tensed up. He could read the pain from her face.

"It is shameful... don't ask me such a question."

Roger didn't know what to say. He could tell that something cruel must have happened to her. Still he wanted to know, but he knew that now was not the proper time.

Before Roger could think of some words, Lili spoke up.

"How long until you know where to go?"

Roger thought for a second and then answered.

"When the next moon is up high will be the time. Then it has been three days."

"Hmm…?" she summed quietly.

"What will you do when the time comes?" he asked.

They still hadn't come far from Spirithelm, but since they have been discovered, there was no reason for them to stay together. Perhaps it would be a favorable solution for both him and her if they went separate ways. Being caught was less likely that way since their pursuers were looking for them as a pair.

She appeared to be deep in thoughts. Then she turned to gaze at him. Her dark eyes swallowed up all light, contrasting the faintly illuminated skin around them. Her lips began to move.

"I don't know," she answered uncomfortably.

"I see."

Roger looked up the church's ceiling. The moonlight scattered around, gently lighting up the top.

Then suddenly he felt a soft touch on his upper legs. His view wandered down.

"Lili?"

She had placed her head on his legs, her tiny hands like paws next to it.

"Just this night," she pleaded. "I'll be the feared demon queen you know when the sun breaks, I promise."

Roger saw tears at the corner of her eyes glittering in the shine. He gently stroked her hair. She reminded him of the cat that had lived alongside him in Brineguard during his childhood years. Lili's hair was at least as soft as the cat's fur back then.

He rested his head on the altar behind him and the

remaining tension left his body. When his eyes wandered down again, he noticed her chest gently moving up and down with each breath. It appeared like the spirits' had taken over.

He closed his eyes as well and waited for the sleep to come.

Roger's eyes opened.

The moonlight had been replaced by a warmer color. The sunrise was about to happen.

He noticed Lili who still reminded him of a cat, though her tail wasn't as cuddly. He carefully placed his hand on her shoulder and shook her a little. Slowly her eyes went halfway open, looking up at him.

"Good morning," he told her.

She just stared back at him, still half asleep. Roger turned to his side and pulled out the two black mantles. One of them he put over Lili.

She let out a weird sound and then seemed to have fully awoken. Her upper body rose and she punched against the mantle from the inside.

"Ah, why is it so dark…?" she called in panic.

Moments after, the mantle came off and her eyes found Roger, in need of an explanation.

Her hair had taken quite a hit being all ruffled at the top.

"Put it on. We better leave sooner than later."

With his legs now free, he stood up and put on the other mantle.

"Your hair is in disorder," she proclaimed.

Roger turned around and gave her an uncertain look. They weren't near such luxuries as a mirror, so he thought she didn't need to know about her own hair and kept quiet instead.

He started walking towards the exit. When he reached the door, he carefully opened it just wide enough that he could make out the scenery outside.

It was still dark enough for them to sneak through the city unseen. As expected, there weren't any guards around the church.

He turned his head in an attempt to remind Lili that they needed to go but lost his composure when she unexpectedly stood right beside him. He stumbled back a step in shock. The black hood pulled over her head didn't help lessen the initial impression.

"Don't surprise me like that..."

She showed him a big smile. "I'm glad demons still trigger an innate reflex within humans."

"I'm feeling more fearful towards the thought that the sun will rise too quickly," he countered, grabbing the door handle and pulling the door open. "Let's go."

Roger led the way to the next side alley with quick steps. They needed to reach the gate before the sun rose fully.

They were running for a few minutes now. Lili spoke up from behind without a hint of exhaustion in her voice.

"Somehow this isn't so bad," she said with a refreshed voice.

Roger was slightly confused on her remark.

"What do you mean?"

"All of this... sneaking around like this..." she answered. "Very different from the war... but we're still surrounded by enemies."

Roger couldn't comprehend her opinion. How could she find something in this dire situation?

"Sure..."

Roger stopped at a corner and carefully looked around. It was one of the main streets through the city. And indeed he saw someone. A single man carrying boxes full of fruits to prepare his stand for the day. Roger waited for the right moment and sneaked past, entering the opposing alley.

"Some humans are quite eager it seems," she commented on the man's early wake.

"I guess some are," he answered plainly.

He gave his full attention to getting through the city without being spotted. Unlike the seemingly unconcerned Lili, he recognized the graveness of the situation.

The city was huge and it didn't help the distance that the church was further from the gate than the inn.

During the time Roger and Lili made their way towards the gate, the sun eventually had surfaced from beneath the walls. It got bright very quickly and more and more people began their work for the day.

At some point, sneaking was no longer an option. They had to blend in with the city folk, posing as mere travelers. Still, Roger preferred side alleys over the main streets.

Eventually, they had reached the street leading to the gate. They were walking through an alley that ran alongside it. More and more horsed wagons with merchants on the driver seat entered the street. All of them had done their business and were heading to their next stop to buy and sell goods.

But merchants weren't the only ones that increased the closer they got to the gates. Roger's uneasiness spiked with every new guard he noticed. There was definitely something going on and he feared that he and Lili were the reason.

Roger realized that they couldn't possibly leave the city by just walking through the gates. The guards surely had been ordered to capture any suspicious pair they encountered. There was only one way he could think of to leave the city unnoticed. Roger suddenly turned around and ran into the other direction.

"Hey! Why are you running away now?"

"They are searching for us. If we get spotted by a guard, it's over. There's no way we could escape the city defense force. We'd be like rats trapped in a cage with a cobra."

"Ha?! Then why are you running away from the gate?"

"I hope it's still there," Roger mumbled, continuing to run.

"Wha—"

Roger interrupted her with a hand gesture, telling her to stop at the corner.

"It's still there," he said, relieved, while looking carefully around the alley corner.

Lili walked next to him and did the same.

"A wagon?"

A wagon was parked in an alley that led into the main street.

"If we got into one of these, we can just roll out the city together with the goods," he told her.

"Oh... I see."

A merchant was loading some goods from the

building next to it into the wagon. Roger waited for him to finish.

"When he starts driving, we need to run," he told Lili.

She replied with a nod.

And then the moment came. The wagon was set into motion and Roger and Lili started running. They quietly entered and moved further in. There were a few wooden crates in the back corner with a bit of space behind them. That's where they decided to hide.

The wagon entered the main street and followed along together with the other wagons. Roger could hear the liveliness that continued to grow outside.

It was crowded inside the wagon. Lili's side was neatly touching his arm. Both of them were facing the end of the wagon, their feet against the wooden crates. If anyone were to look inside the wagon, the crates would shield Roger and Lili from their vision.

The wagon drove for a few minutes until it suddenly came to a halt. They stood there for too long for it to be just a crowded street. Roger turned around, careful not make any sound, and took a glimpse of outside through a gap between the wagon structure and the cover shielding the goods from the weather.

Roger saw the gate. They were close, but something was off. Dozens of wagons of other merchants had pilled up before the gate. The guards from earlier had been replaced by full-fledged knights that were patrolling the place. Under the gate a bundle of knights blocked the exit.

The gate should have been open at this time of the day. The sun was hastily making its way to the top. But nobody could leave or enter the city. The knights stationed there seemed to have no intention of letting even a rat through.

Roger turned back around, facing the crates.

"What's wrong?" Lili asked, whispering.

"They're blocking the gates."

Her eyes widened.

"Because of us?"

"Probably."

There was no doubt that the spectacle outside was due to their presence. Roger bit on his teeth. What was going to happen now? Would they block the gates for as long as they didn't find them? If so, there was no way they could leave the city. But even at this realization there was no turning back. The place swarmed with knights and leaving the wagon now would undoubtably lead to their discovery.

"What are we going to do?" Lili asked, interrupting his thoughts.

He looked at her in surprise and thought of an answer.

"We'll probably be fine. They can't risk becoming the target of all the merchants' anger. At some point they need to clear the way," he assured her.

Those words were Roger's attempt of making the situation sound better than it was. He tried to convince himself that his words would come true.

Roger flinched when he heard an unfamiliar voice close by, coming from the outside.

"Excuse me. Could you tell me why we are waiting?" a man's voice said from the front of the wagon. It seemed to be the merchant driving the wagon.

Roger heard footsteps coming closer. The jangling

armor, the iron hitting the stone ground, it was undoubtably a knight that neared.

"We've received word that there's a pair of a Seeker and a demon hiding in the city. That's why the city has been sealed off," the knight answered dutiful.

"A Seeker and a demon you say? Surely, you're jesting, Sir!" The merchant laughed.

"I'm afraid that isn't the case. There has been an incident in a town to the east involving both a Seeker and a demon. A messenger sent us word about it and yesterday's night three guards had encountered them. They are still in the city, Sir."

A moment of silence passed by. Then the merchant answered.

"It's always those Seekers that bring misfortune upon us modest men. Curse them!" he spit out.

"Ha! Agreed!" The knight laughed. "Wait until this bastard is caught! We'll be making sure, he'll meet an end worthy of a Seeker." His voice was filled with schadenfreude.

"Surely the dryness this summer was one of theirs doing. Only death deserves them," the merchant answered.

The mood had changed. The earlier lightness was replaced by hatred. It leaked out of their mouths in waves.

"I assure you, Sir. When I meet him, I'll be sure to take his eyes. He has no need for those, darkness is all that awaits him," the knights continued.

Roger calmly listened to their conversation. Their words didn't affect him. If he wasn't prepared to endure such cheap badmouthing, he wouldn't have come far.

But it wasn't the same for his companion. He had noticed a trembling sensation on his arm. Her face induced a bit of fear inside him. The eyes had started dying red and from her clenched teeth he could see sharp fangs that weren't there before.

"Lili, calm down," he whispered. He couldn't have her go out of control now. "Everything's alright," he assured her.

Lili's trembling came to a halt and she looked at him.

"Alright, you say?! Have you gone deaf?" she whispered angrily.

"Let them say what they want. If we are discovered now, there's no tomorrow."

The merchant continued.

"Have you prepared the ritual?"

Roger realized that Lili shouldn't hear what they were about to say. He took his hands and quickly pressed them against Lili's ears.

"Surely! All seven days worth. By the seventh, he'll be sure to have lost his mind. It'll be unworldly pain that only Seekers will know," the knight declared proudly.

"Such greatness! I see he'll be in good hands."

"And there's even a ritual for the demon. The priest was so kind to tell us about it. Apparently it was used a thousand years ago for the last captured demons," the knight told.

"Oh! I'll be sure to return to hear about it in detail."

This was as far as Roger could go. Lili had freed herself of his hands and looked at him angrily. He put his hands together and bowed in an apologetic manner. When he opened his eyes again, he saw the same angry face as before. Demons seemed to have different conventions for expressing apology, he concluded.

But something had caught his attention during their conversation. They had prepared a ritual for Lili, one that was used a thousand years ago. What was powerful enough to hold back a demon that possessed monstrous strength? Roger had no idea. He couldn't imagine that any human could stop a demon.

"I have to return to my post now. It seems they have started the inspections. A great day I wish," the knight said to the merchant, resuming his post.

"God's blessings on you!" the merchant encountered.

Their conversation had ended.

Roger turned around to take a glimpse of outside again. His fears turned out to be true. The wagons in front of him were inspected by knights one by one. Soon it would be their turn.

He looked at Lili. She had realized the situation they were in. She just stared nervously at the wooden crate in front of her. Roger followed to do the same.

After some time another knight approached the merchant.

"I'm tasked to inspect your goods, Sir," the knight said.

"Go ahead. I've got no Seeker to hide! Ha-ha-ha!"

Roger's eyes followed the sounds of the knight's footsteps circling the wagon. Then the knight had arrived at the back. Moments passed and the knight just walked back to the merchant without entering the wagon.

"Everything seems to be in proper shape. Good luck in your trade."

"Thank you. I hope you find the Seeker!"

Roger felt relieved. They survived the inspections without an incident. But Lili wasn't relieved. Her anger had returned. He wondered why that was. They only badmouthed him. But Lili's anger wasn't as severe as earlier. He decided to leave her and wait until the wagon had passed the gate.

After some time, the wagon started moving again until it made a final halt at what must have been the gate.

"We need to inspect your goods, Sir," another knight said.

"My goods were inspected already," the merchant encountered, surprised.

"I'm afraid that's what our orders are, Sir."

"It can't be helped then, go ahead."

Roger's heart started beating profoundly. They just survived one inspection, why was there a second one?

He and Lili remained as quiet as the dead while a knight circled around the wagon once again. This time however, the knight stepped into the wagon. Roger could hear him moving some of the goods around. The inspection was on an entirely different level than the one earlier. *Thorough* didn't even meet justice to what was happening.

After every inspected good, the knight came closer to the crates. Roger thought through the options he had. But there were none. He couldn't think of any way out. They were surrounded by knights and he was no match for any of them. Was this the end? Perhaps it was his fate for letting a demon accompany him. Lili... ever since he encountered her, his life had changed tremendously.

The knight now stood in front of the crates, directly on the other side. But before he could move them, he flew out of the wagon in the blink of an eye and landed several meters away on the ground with the crate smashing open on top of him.

Roger slowly turned his head towards Lili who was now standing. Her eyes were a deep red, the same as that night. Her fangs from earlier were running up and down her lips. He felt fear. This was a being of insurmountable power no human could ever comprehend. She stood so close to him, but yet he felt that he wouldn't reach her even if he stretched out his arm.

Seconds later, clattering sound emerged from all around the wagon and the fabric covering it tore open. A dozen of spears pierced the inside, followed by a panicking cry from the merchant. Roger closed his eyes in reflex.

When he opened them again, he saw the sharp metal hanging over him being pulled back to the outside. Along with it he spotted Lili. Several spears had penetrated her small body more than halfway through. When the spears were pulled back, blood shot out from her wounds and she coughed up some more, painting her fangs red. Her body collapsed like a corpse and she fell backwards with her head hitting the wooden structure next to him. A lake of blood spread beneath her, eyes closed, her body lifeless.

"No..." Roger cried out. "It can't be..."

He reached out with his hand and stroked over her cheeks. They were still warm, but he felt that the warmth wouldn't remain for too long.

She just lay there like a sleeping doll. The blood she had lost was more than what he though would fit inside her small body. "Why...?" he asked himself, or perhaps the world. She had lost everything and was sealed for over a thousand years. The last remaining demon, a demon queen, and now she lay in a sea of blood before him. Was this how it would end? Was this everything he could do for her? And would he follow her soon?

He made a decision. He'd take revenge for her and if it was the last thing he did. He took out his knife from his bag and gripped it hard with both hands. His eyes must have been even more fearsome than what Lili could manage. He looked at the knights that were slowly nearing from the back of the wagon, their spears pointed at them.

He held his small knife against the massive spears. He was prepared to kill. No matter the odds, he'll take some of them with him.

He stood up, still in the corner, and took a step forward. But the knights had stopped. Their faces were filled with fear and doubt.

"M-monster..." one of them called out.

Roger turned his head to where the knights were looking. It was Lili. Slowly her body rose from the ground, her wounds vanishing quickly.

"Such shame... it seems I haven't yet full awakened from my slumber. A thousand years ago I wouldn't have collapsed from something like this," she declared, brushing off the incident as an everyday occurrence.

She took a few steps forward. Her back was facing him then.

"I apologize for ruining the clothes you bought so kindly."

Roger couldn't muster the words to answer.

The knights had started approaching again, more

slowly than before. Roger could feel her demonic power leaking from her body. Then she spun around at inhuman speeds and kicked some of the remaining goods at the knights who followed the same fate as the first.

In the next instant her wings grew, ripping through the black mantle and became thrice their initial size. A pressure wave blew off the wagon's covers, revealing the baffled knights that surrounded them, a dozen right, a dozen left. Each were in full armor and holding a mighty spear. Some of their spears had a tip dyed in deep red. All of them were paralyzed.

But what kept his attention were the enormously large wings that had spread out in front of him.

"You truly are a demon," he uttered. "Are you going to fly?"

"I will," she answered.

Roger felt the same as before. She was close, yet so far. He felt insecure from her answer. Would she take him with her? Could she even carry his weight with those wings? He had no doubt that they would take her to the skies, but he had to weight double at least. She turned around and looked him in the eyes with an expression he had never seen before. Somehow serious, somehow sad.

The next instant, he saw her charging at him. His eyes closed. When he opened them again, he could see the knights running after them getting smaller and smaller. He was in the air. He was flying. Flying with…

"…Lili," he mumbled.

She held him under his arms with her tiny hands. She gazed forward.

"I thought you would leave me behind to die," Roger confessed.

Her expression didn't change.

"Don't assume I'm evil just because I'm a demon," she said. "My race has lived together for thousands of years. That wouldn't have been possible if we were busy plotting evil."

Roger let out a chuckle.

"Truly..." he said, smiling.

"Even though you are a human, you've done a lot for me. You were the one who lifted my seal, bought me food and even clothes. I've caused you a lot of trouble. As a queen, I have to make sure to pay you back, otherwise that would add to my pile of shame I already have."

Roger smiled. He looked at the tiny knights in front of the tiny gate and city walls. They were no different than ants by now.

And so, Roger and Lili flew off into the distance.

Chapter 3

Lili had flown them far into the nearest forest and landed at a small clearing. The distance was far enough so that they wouldn't encounter the knights very soon.

Lili bowed down before a tree, using her arm as support and panted heavily.

"Are you ok?" Roger asked.

"…don't…worry…" she answered between her breaths. "I'm ok."

Roger was surprised by how much stamina it took her to fly. But what did Roger know about flying? He didn't have wings sprouting from his back to experience it himself.

Soon her breaths became lighter. Then she suddenly stamped on the ground angrily.

"How do they dare?" she shouted. "Those lowly humans taking me lightly, ignoring me outright," she complained furiously.

Roger now realized why she had made such a face in the wagon. The merchant and the knight had hurt her pride.

She turned around. Her face was a mixture of anger and the threat of tears.

"Do I not look frightening enough?" she asked. "Are you saying I'm less frightening than you, a Seeker?"

Roger looked at her. She was like a child throwing a tantrum. Her eyes, wings and teeth had returned to normal. She now looked just like a twelve year-old girl. Not very frightening indeed, but he couldn't tell her that.

"You surely look frightening, more so than a Seeker. I can barely stand, see?" Roger pointed at his legs. They still were shaking from earlier when they were surrounded by knights.

Her eyes turned slim and she looked at Roger in disappointment. She quickly closed the distance with large steps and drove Roger backwards until his back met a tree. But she didn't stop there. Her face became closer and Roger slid down the bark until his bottom hit the ground. Her face was dangerously close, just like that night in the church.

"Do I really look frightening?" she asked, unconvinced.

He avoided her big, dark eyes.

"It is certainly frightening how you violate my personal space."

She pulled her face back and turned around.

"Unbelievable. Do I look so harmless that you would try to fool me?"

"I don't think you need to look frightening. You look fine as you are," he said plainly.

She didn't answer.

"Lili?"

She didn't answer still. Instead, after some while, she turned around and said, "Let's go."

Her anger had left her face somehow.

Roger rose, brushing off the remains of dirt on his clothes and started walking.

"Let's do that," he said.

And so, both of them were walking in the opposite direction they came from. If they stayed where they had landed, it would be an easy task for the knights to find them.

"Lili?"

"Hm?"

"Earlier... how did your wounds heal so quickly?"

Her eyes widened for a moment and then quickly returned to normal.

"Oh, of course, you don't know," she said. "I'm sort of special among demons. I have something called a supreme queen attribute. For males it's called supreme king attribute."

Roger looked at her curiously.

"Demons with this attribute are immortal," she declared as if it was nothing.

"Immortal, you say?! You mean, no matter what happens to you, you won't die?"

"True. That's the curse of immortality, although I didn't live long enough to experience that yet."

"Didn't you say you were more than three hundred years—"

Lili moved through a bunch of branches and when they snapped back in place, Roger barely evaded them.

He moved through.

It was still hard to believe that the small girl walking in front of him was a demon queen, and immortal on top of that.

Slightly salty, she stopped and turned her head, throwing him a look of displeasure. She spoke up.

"Demons have longer lifespans than humans. A typical demon lives three hundred years, a king or queen a thousand and I forever."

Roger knew that demons had a longer life span than humans, but he didn't know that even among them some were different.

"How does one become a king or queen?"

They continued walking.

"It's decided on birth. A child that is not under the influence of a king or queen will receive the king or queen attribute. Every other child born after that will be under its influence and not be born with that attribute," she explained. "However, a king or queen only influences a limited area around them. Here in this realm there could be born but a few kings and queens."

Roger chuckled in irony. It was similar for humans, yet different. A human king would be born as a king also, but only those closest to the current king, his offspring, would be born as such.

"What so funny?"

"No, nothing," he answered. "Just thinking about how kings are born in the human realm."

She looked at him confused.

"Then how did you receive your supreme queen attribute?"

She gazed at the forest ground before her.

"My father had the king attribute and my mother the queen attribute."

Somehow she seemed sad, but Roger couldn't tell why.

The demon race seemed far more complicated than the tales gave it credit. Thinking about it, he remembered her absurdly long name.

"Do all demons have a name as long as yours?" he asked. "Yours was Liliesh Zeka…" He was thinking hard how the rest of it was but was interrupted by Lili.

"Liliesh Zeka Elralloth Ariestyse Erthroriach," she completed. "Demons' names always have five parts. The personal name, secondary female stem, secondary male stem, primary female stem, primary male stem."

She looked at him for a moment, reading his confused expression.

"Erthroriach is the primary male stem of my father, and Ariestyse is the primary female stem of my mother. Elralloth is the primary female stem of my father, and Zeka is the primary male stem of my mother. And Liliesh is my personal name."

"That sounds very complicated."

"Perhaps humans are just too simple to understand," she said suggestively. "But it really isn't that hard if you know how important stems are in the demon world. Your stems determine your stamina, size of wings, length of tail and the glow of your eyes. To honor those stems they are given to the child's name. My child would carry on both Ariestyse and Erthroriach. And its child would carry on Ariestyse if my child was female and Erthroriach if it was male. That's why the most important families usually will have both male and female children to carry on their stems."

"It's surprisingly similar to humans. Your birth decides your social status. If you're born poor, you'll be working your entire life, but if you're born into nobility, the work will be done for you," Roger said. "And for the royal family it is important to have both a male successor to the throne and a princess that can be married off into nobility. Is your family the same? Do you have siblings?"

"No, I don't," she said plainly.

Roger was surprised. Lili seemed to be of a very important family with her parents both being king and queen. He wondered why she didn't have any siblings then.

"Have you any then?" she asked.

"No."

"I see. Then we have something in common," she said, somehow happily.

"Besides running from the knights you mean?"

She let out a chuckle.

"That might be true," she said, smiling. "Say, are you lonely?" she asked all of a sudden.

It would be preposterous to claim the life of a Seeker not lonely and he had no reason to hide this from her.

"It's hard sometimes, but liberating at others, I guess?"

"Liberating? How so?"

Roger thought back to his childhood days.

"I occasionally remember my village and the people there I left. Each time I wonder how they are doing and if they'd forgive me if I returned at the end of my journey," Roger began. "But traveling and seeing the world isn't so bad and with the resentment towards

Seekers, I'd rather stay away from common people."

"Your village, you say... how was it like?"

Roger was surprised that she suddenly took such interest in him.

"Its name is Brineguard. A small village in the small territory Ashana. It houses just a few families and there were a few children my age that I called my friends. We had fresh water from a clear and gentle river, wide plains of grass and a forest close by. Most of the adults were working as farmers, and that also should have been my designated work, but now I ended up here."

"Hm... Brineguard, a fine village it seems. I'm kind of interested in this place now," she said. "Say, when your journey ends and the demon race is resurrected, will you show me there?"

Roger looked at her in surprise. Her face voice was filled with honesty and good intentions. If someone told him a month ago that he'd be having a conversation with a demon like this, he would have sent them to the church, praying for their cure.

He smiled. "Sure, I'd be happy to!"

If his journey really ended someday, he'd want to return to his village and meet his friends. And if he brought Lili with him, at least he had something to tell.

The two of them continued to walk through the forest. Eventually, the darkness slowly shrouded the forest, and they decided to set up camp for the night. Continuing further would have been madness.

The night arrived quickly and both lay down to sleep.

Roger opened his eyes. Soft rays of light entered, but his vision was shaking, like the earth trembled. Slowly the senses came to him.

"Hey! Wake up!" a voice called to him. "Wake up, I say!"

He looked up and saw Lili.

"I'm awake. You can stop shaking me now," he said, irritated.

"The knights are approaching."

Roger suddenly was on high alert and sat up straight. He looked around a few times, but he couldn't sense the presence of anyone other than Lili.

"You can tell?"

"Sure, I can. For me it was war a few days ago, remember?"

Contrary to her words she seemed to be rather calm.

"Where—"

Roger's words stopped in his throat. He closed his eyes. He saw a faint light in the distance surrounded by darkness. A light that drew him closer, that tempted him with his sweet flickering. It was time. The break from his life as a Seeker had ended.

"What's wrong?" Lili asked.

"Nothing, I just know the location of the next spell now."

"And where is it then? Hopefully not in this direction," she said, pointing in the direction they came from.

"Is that were the knights are drawing closer?"

She nodded.

"Then we have to hurry. I'll tell you on the way."

Roger stood up.

He was scared by the thought that the knights had caught up to them so quickly, though according to Lili they still were quite a distance away and seemed to be unaware of their exact location.

They continued their way through the forest, hurrying away from the chasing knights.

"So, where is it now?" Lili asked pressingly.

"Oh, the spell? It's both a curse and a blessing. It will give an end to the chase, but the way will by hard," he told her. "It's in Ehoya, the elven realm."

Her mouth widened until she bit her teeth together forcefully.

"Ha?! Those cowardly elves? Hiding behind trees and shooting arrows with their ludicrous bows..." she raged, making Roger imagine what would happen if they encountered an elf on the way. "And their long-distance magic..."

She didn't seem to have the best experience with elves. And Roger couldn't tell if she was right. He had never met a full-fledged elf, only halfs that resided in the human realm and they were, as most halfs, in chains working as slaves.

"Don't worry, it won't be so soon before you see one," he assured her. "The elves have isolated themselves from other races. You won't see them anywhere else."

"They still claim the same realm I suppose?"

"I've never heard that any of the races changed their realm after the war, so I suppose they do."

"Then how are you going to get there? The sea's in between and they still appear to be as repellant as a thousand years ago," she said in disgust.

"That is indeed the challenging part, but not impossible. There's a ship that fares to an island called

Crystalreach in the Asmein territory. The territory consists of several islands away from the mainland, and Crystalreach is closest to the elven realm," he told her. "But before that we need to enter Strosa, a major port city where this ship docks. It's not that far away."

"We just escaped the last city and now you want to enter a new one?" she asked sarcastically, fully aware of their circumstances.

"I don't plan on getting discovered," he said. "That also means no feast for you," he countered, visibly hitting a weak spot.

She covered her upper body with her arms and looked at him in disbelieve.

"You don't intend to starve me out, do you?"

"You're immortal, right? You can get by a few days without food, I assume."

"Being immortal doesn't make you unable to feel hunger. And you better not want to experience my hungry self."

Roger didn't need to start imagining to know she was right.

"Should I fly us?" she asked suddenly. "It'll be faster that way."

"The risk someone sees us is too high. As long as we stay in the protection of the forest, our chasers won't catch up."

Lili lowered her head in disappointment.

"I'm sure there will be anoth—"

In place of his words was a moan full of agony. He felt a piercing pain in his right shoulder, greater than anything he had experienced so far. Suddenly his vision turned up to the sky until his back hit the hard ground.

He saw a wooden stick emerging from his shoulder. It was an arrow. He didn't need to pull it out to know that it was metal coated. His blood vessels thumped in alternation with the pain.

The next moment he was hit by a familiar shockwave. Lili had spread her wings out mightily, her tail erect and her fangs ready to devour her prey. She was like the wrath itself.

Another arrow came flying, but it didn't reach. Before it could, she crushed it to dust with her bare hands.

To their front, an arc of knights rose from the cover of the forest. Some had hidden behind trees, some under bushes. They were fully equipped with sturdy metal as armor and a hand full of crossbows and razor sharp swords. They blocked the way in a half-moon formation, their eyes ready to kill.

Without exchanging a word the crossbowmen fired another round of arrows at the raging demon. With a short flutter of her wings, the arrows stopped mid-air, falling to the forest ground. The swordsmen unsheathed their blades and readied themselves for combat.

The crossbowmen were loading another set of arrows when their eyes froze. A fountain of blood entered their vision and one of their men collapsed to the ground. Before that man stood Lili, covered in red. She had pierced his heart with her bare hands. Their armor didn't stop her in the slightest.

At this moment she looked just like the demons Roger knew from the tales, deadly manslaughterers no human stood a chance.

After the first another followed and collapsed in a lake of his own blood. Roger could feel the fear the knights leaked into the forest. Their legs were shaking, their grip unsteady. None of their arrows or swords had a chance to reach Lili before she reached them.

In the blink of an eye she covered the scene in red until the last remaining knights had lost their will to fight and struggled with their weak legs away. But Lili showed no mercy. She slaughtered them one after another, even though they had long surrendered.

Roger gathered his strength.

"LILI!" he cried out. "It's enough," he added and she stopped.

One man was all that was still moving. He stumbled away through the thicket, eventually vanishing in the cover of the forest.

He saw Lili turning around, coated in red, her eyes burning with wrath. Then his vision went blurry and darkness followed.

When he opened his eyes again, he sat leaning against the rough bark of a tree. The nightmarish scene filled with lifeless bodies and the stench of death was spread out next to him. Lili was crouching before him, holding a piece of her coat his her hands. Her expression was one of conflict.

"Lili…"

She quickly turned her head and looked at him. She had gone back to normal, her eyes dark and wings small. Only the blood-stained parts on her face and coat were the unmistakable prove that it was her that caused that scene.

"Don't worry, I'll treat your wound," she said, uncharacteristically for a demon.

Roger let out a pained chuckle and forced a smiled. The thought that a demon was about to treat his wounds filled him with laughter. He saw her again taking an unstained part of her coat in her hands, hesitating. Now he realized why she did.

"Look in my bag at the front. There are bandages."

She did as told and quickly found them in a separate pocket. Some minimal equipment for treating wounds was a necessity. Especially when he was traveling alone.

He used his undamaged left hand and grabbed the arrow still stuck in his right shoulder. He bit his teeth together and pulled it out forcibly. A pain ten times worse than what he felt when he was hit shuddered through his body.

"What are you doing?!" Lili shouted. "Be a bit more careful with your body. Unlike mine it doesn't regenerate quickly."

"I hardly could leave it were it was," he encountered with a pained voice.

Without answering Lili gave him her undivided attention and first helped him undress his coat and then proceeded wrapping around the bandage he gave her.

After some time she had finished.

"I'm in your debt," he said.

"No… it is my fault that this arrow hit you. I wasn't paying attention," she said, avoiding her gaze.

Roger remembered what happened just moments ago, when he was hit by the arrow and when the massacre began. She didn't have to kill those who had lost their will to fight, he thought. But what say did he have in the matter? Talking things out with the knights was hardly an option and judging her, a demon queen, for slaughtering knights that were out to kill them would be arrogant at best.

"Please don't ever kill innocents, only those who are ready to kill," he pleaded her, hoping that in the future no tragedy would occur.

She looked at him in surprise.

"It is not my amusement to kill, not during the war, not now," she answered. "However," she continued. "To those that threaten the lives of those under my protection, I show no mercy."

Roger's eyes widened. "I'm under your protection?"

"You thought you are not?" She chuckled. "Although you're not a fellow demon, you are the only one that knows of my fate. As long as I'm following you around, you're under my protection."

She lowered her head looking to the side, her eyes uncomfortably slim.

"But as you can see, I couldn't protect my race, nor could I protect you."

"That's not true," Roger said. "If it were just me against the knights, I wouldn't have lived seconds."

But Lili just turned her head away and stood up.

"Can you walk?"

Roger rose from the ground. A stinging pain made him remember the state his shoulder was in. He wouldn't be able to fight with his right arm. He hoped that it wouldn't come down to it.

"My legs are of no concern," he answered, imagining what would have happened if they had hit one of them.

"We are still being chased," she said.

"I guessed that. Those knights weren't from Prok. Strosa already knows about us."

"But we still need to go?"

"We do. It's the only way."

Roger carefully took the first steps, making his way through the corpses. Lili followed closely after and both of them continued their way to Strosa.

"I won't let them kill you," Lili promised, breaking the silence.

Roger laughed sarcastically. "They wouldn't kill me. At least not here."

Lili looked at him quizzically. "What do you mean?"

"They would capture me and conduct the ritual awaiting all Seekers that have been caught," he began. "It's a torture that lasts one week, doubling the pain each day and ending in death at the seventh."

Lili looked disgusted. "Despicable. Why would they do this?"

"It just shows how hated Seekers are in this world."

"Of all the races, humans sure are the most disgraceful."

"But there are those who do not like the way Seekers are treated. I haven't met any, but I've heard there are," he encountered.

"Perhaps humans are also the most versatile."

Roger and Lili continued their way and Lili noted after some time that their chasers from Prok have strayed off path.

Eventually, the night drew closer and Roger set up a camp with a fire.

He sat down and watched the flames. Lili sat on the opposing side just like the night when he first met her.

He thought about the ambush that had brought him

injury. He really hadn't thought that Strosa already knew about them. They had to be very careful from now on. It would be best to take the soonest ship to Crystalreach. He didn't know how long they had to wait otherwise and with so many knights as enemies, he certainly didn't want to imagine how they would spend this excess time.

Roger's thoughts were brought back by the crackling of the flame.

He looked at Lili on the other side. She just quietly stared at the fire. Perhaps she was thinking about her race, the future and the past. He could imagine there was a lot she had to think about.

He remembered her waking him up this morning. He wondered how she could sense their chasers that were a far distance away while missing the ones that led the ambush.

"Lili?" he called out across the fire.

"Hm?"

She raised her head and looked at him.

"Can demons feel the presence of others?" he asked. "You know... when you woke me up this morning."

"It's not like I have a sixth sense or anything, my ears are just good," she answered, putting up a smile.

"You could hear them? From such a distance? Then why did you miss the knights at the ambush?"

At this moment Roger realized that he had asked the wrong question. Her smiled had vanished and was replaced by an expression of guilt.

"It wasn't your fault," Roger added, hoping to relieve her.

"No, I think I could have noticed them if I had payed more attention," she answered, still overcome with guilt.

"I can hear things that stand out like clattering armor among whistling leaves, but I can't hear each leaf that falls to the ground."

"I see," Roger encountered. "Quite impressive."

Lili threw him a doubtful expression over the flames.

"Every demon could do that."

"I think it's still impressive," Roger said. "I'm a bit jealous. Having such good hearing would certainly help."

Lili started laughing for a moment.

"You're an odd one."

Then her expression changed. She looked like she was hesitating.

"How's your shoulder?"

Roger hid a smirk. Maybe he was odd, but a demon that worried about his shoulder was a whole other oddity.

"It hurt more than anything I've ever experienced, but I can almost not feel it now. The arrow didn't seem to have reached the bone," he answered. "Perhaps in a few days it's as good as new."

"I see," she said. "Then… can I ask you a selfish favor?"

A demon asking him of a favor? Perhaps the day long chase and the ambush was getting to them. He could certainly feel the exhaustion, but he didn't know about Lili.

"If it's something I can do."

"Can you bind my hair with the ribbons then," she asked, almost shyly. "If your shoulder allows it."

Roger was surprised. He had bought the ribbons to hide her long hair, but it seemed like she actually liked them.

But there was something else that made him hesitate.

He felt tremendous guilt for pretending to know how to put the ribbons to use and ended up leading to their discovery at the inn. He couldn't bear this cross any longer.

"I'm sorry," he said, bowing low. "At the inn, it was my first time with those ribbons. I only ever saw them on some girls in Brineguard."

Then after a moment of pause, he heard laughing emerge from the other side and looked up.

"Don't be concerned," she said. "I can't use them at all. It would be a shame to buy them and not put them to use."

Roger rose his head in relief.

"Then if that's ok with you..."

"It is," she encountered promptly.

She stood up energetically and moved over to his side and stopped in front of him with her back facing him.

Roger's view was filled with a curtain of black. He took the ribbons out of his bag and stood up as well.

"How do you want it?"

"Don't ask me. I've spent my entire life with my hair like this."

Roger thought for a moment, trying to come up with an idea. It had to be something that even he could do and would leave some satisfaction for her.

"Ok, I think I have an idea."

"Go ahead."

On her command he took her hair at her neck and sorted it into two even tails. He bundled one of them with his hand and put the first ribbon around with the other. He made a loop and pulled it tight. He repeated the same for the other side.

He took a step back and looked at her. In his humble opinion it didn't look too bad, but he was certain no girl would be proud of him for his feat.

"I'm done," he told Lili.

She swung around a few times with a face full of expectations, trying to chase her hair. Then she stopped and showed him a smile.

"I commend you," she said, convinced. "This time it seems to hold," she added with a teasing smile.

To Roger, that comment was entirely unnecessary.

"I'm glad you like it."

Lili proceeded to turn around another few times, her hair following her every turn.

Roger noticed her tail waving along similarly to her hair. He realized that he actually never had looked closer at her tail, or her wings for that matter. The only demon attribute he was quite familiar with were her eyes.

"You think you can do me a favor as well?" Roger asked.

She stopped turning in surprise and looked at him curiously.

"I guess I do owe you one," she admitted. "What do you ask of me?"

Roger put up a smile.

"Can I touch your wings and tail?"

By that time he was fairly convinced that the day was getting to him.

Lili stumbled back a few steps, holding her tail in protection.

"W-why would you ask that?" she asked, flabbergasted. Her face had turned a slight red.

"Is it not ok?" Roger asked in confusion.

She just returned a blushful look and didn't answer.

Roger sat down defeated.

"I should have touched them while I carried her out of church," he murmured to himself while staring at the fire.

When he looked back at Lili, he saw her avoiding his gaze, looking shyly at the ground.

"It's…" he heard her whispering.

But her voice was too quiet for him to hear everything.

Then she looked at him again, uneasy. She then walked to his front and sat herself down, facing the fire.

"It's only because you did me a favor," she argued.

"Does that mean it's ok?"

"It is."

Roger didn't believe she would agree to this after her initial reaction. He wondered why she was so flustered about it.

"Then…" he said before starting.

He carefully took his hands and placed them on the top of her wings.

He noticed Lili twitching a little.

He then slid his fingers sideways. They had a soft fuzz at the top but a sturdy frame. He moved his fingers further down. The wings now became thinner and grew multiple birds worth of feathers but didn't lose in their fuzzy softness.

He felt satisfied with the wings and removed his hands.

"How was it?" she asked suddenly.

"They were soft."

"…I see."

"Now the tail?" she asked in a slightly hesitant voice.

She moved her tail up between him and her wings.

Roger raised his hand in anticipation. He wondered how it would feel. Unlike her wings he could see no fuzz.

He grabbed the middle of the tail with one hand.

Lili let out a quiet shriek as the twitched forward.

"Be gentle with a demon's tail," she complained reproachfully.

"I'll keep that in mind."

He carefully opened his hand and touched her tail with his fingertips. His fingers followed the tail further to the top. Lili again twitched and let out a weird noise.

There wasn't any fuzz nor fur, but it didn't feel smooth. It had a rough texture. The tail resisted the movement of his fingers as he slid them over.

As he squeezed his fingers a bit, he felt the tail's sturdiness. It didn't deform like the fuzz of her wings, but the texture made it feel soft either way.

He slowly moved his fingers to the heart-shaped tip. When he reached it, he heard yet another noise of Lili. She leaned forward and used her hands as support. She was breathing heavily as her chest moved up and down.

Roger concluded that for the sake of his survival, it was time to conclude this favor of her.

He removed his hands and told her, "I'm done."

Her tail stood up in the air and didn't move from the spot.

"Lili?" he asked carefully.

After she didn't answer, Roger moved to her side to see what was wrong.

He saw her panting heavily, her cheeks dyed in red, but it was different from when she was drunk. She slowly turned her head and looked at him in despair.

"I can't get married now," she exaggerated. She had forming tears at the corners of her eyes.

"Do demons even marry?"

"They do!" she answered in protest.

Somehow it felt very satisfying seeing her like this. She looked somehow very unlike a demon, yet very alike.

"Could it be that the tail is the weak point of a demon?"

Roger flinched back a bit after receiving an angry glare.

"It's not!" she said. "It's just very sensitive."

Roger wondered if that was how demons were defeated during the war but quickly shoved that ridiculous thought away.

"We're even now," she said, throwing a look that suggested only a single possible answer.

"We are," Roger admitted.

Roger wondered what he had been doing for the last few minutes. He noticed that his eyes became heavier. Perhaps he was simply too tired.

"It's getting late," Roger told her, lying down on his right side out of habit but quickly remembered his shoulder and moved to the other side.

"I suppose that's true."

He saw her lying down as well, at the same spot where she had sat for some time now.

Roger's eye became heavier and eventually he drifted off.

Roger was woken by soft sun rays that made it through the forest cover.

He pushed himself off the ground and opened his eyes fully. The fire had burned out and only a pile of ash was remaining.

He took a glimpse of the sleeping queen next to him. As he spotted her tail, he thought of grabbing it shortly but quickly thought better of it.

Instead, he shook her on her shoulder.

"Wake up," he said.

Shortly after, Lili opened her eyes and rose.

"Moaw—ning," she said as she erupted midway into a yawn.

"Can you hear any knights?"

Luckily, she shook her head.

"Then let's go," he told her, rising. "We should hurry."

Lili rose as well and both started walking.

After some time Roger and Lili had reached the end of the forest.

They stood on a hill which flattened into fertile lands with a river dividing them into two parts. The majestic stone walls of Strosa were visible in the distance on the other side of the river.

Careful of any ambush that might await them, Roger scanned the open plains from the hilltop.

The crops looked considerably well if he compared them to the dry dust further to the east. More so, they were high enough to shield a straight man from curious onlookers.

"Let's take the route through the fields," Roger decided.

He took a glance at her after she didn't respond for a while. Her dark eyes were almost sparkling as they wandered through the wide fields. Perhaps most she had seen of the human realm was mountains of lifeless bodies and debris of what had been hard-built structures. He could only imagine, but he was glad that there was no war at this time.

"Impressive, huh?"

She gave a delayed nod. "Truly…"

"Then let's go! You don't need to stand there. You can look at it up close."

"Fool! It's precisely this distance that makes it so astounding," she proclaimed promptly.

Somehow now she sounded more like a queen than her childish self at the market. He remembered that she had lived through more than three hundred years. Maybe such differences in personality happen after living for that long, he thought.

"What about the knights? Have they caught up?" he asked, joining her in her admiration.

"No knight has been near in recent times."

"I see."

Roger was relieved to hear that. At least he now could focus on finding a safe way into the city and not worry about swords that threatened to pierce his back.

"If we don't hurry, it's going to get dark before we reach Strosa. I can assure you that sleeping out in the plains is not an option."

"I guess it can't be helped. Lead the way!"

Roger started walking downhill, the shortest path to the golden crop field. Lili followed him happily.

"Say, you said there's an end to your journey, Seeker's Dream, was it?" she asked on the way down.

"I did, although there's no guarantee that it's true," he

answered. "What about it?"

Roger pushed the first crops to the side and set his foot in between. It was about as tall as he was, but if he tried, he could take a peek over it.

"If you find it... what will you wish for?"

Roger heard the soft sizzling of crops she stepped on from behind.

"I don't know. I haven't thought about it much. It'll probably take a long time if not forever to reach it."

They slowly made their path through the field. Somehow, pushing the flourishing crops aside left a pleasant feeling.

"But it will grant you any wish! There has to be something you desire, surely!"

"I'm not sure."

He felt the warm sun rays shining on his face. The gentle wind made for a cooling alternation.

"Are you not unsatisfied with your life as a Seeker?"

"I'm really not sure...," he answered. "But if you want me to point out the major downside to my life, it would be living isolation. No friends, no family, no one would involve themselves with a Seeker."

"Then you want to life with other humans?"

"If my journey ever ends, I'd like to live the rest of my days like a normal man would. Living in a quiet village with few people and perhaps a wife and a few children, but nothing that would require a great wish to be made."

He heard some chuckling from behind.

"What's so amusing?" he asked, slightly reproachful.

"No, no," she said, still laughing. "I just thought that such a life is not what one imagined after having met you."

Roger wondered if she was mocking him or not, but nonetheless he felt slightly affected.

He turned around and took a look at her. She was holding her stomach and was bent over at the waist. Her long hair waved along her laughter like festive banners in the wind.

"Do I not seem like I could live a normal life?"

She slowly calmed down. "I was just surprised. But I understand. Living a life as you spoke might not be so bad. It's not a lonely life at least!" she said, smiling at him. "You're strong."

"What do you mean? How am I strong?" he asked, confused.

He turned back around to his front and made his way further into the field.

"It's just been a few days since I was unsealed and I can already feel the loneliness nagging on me. I really could be the last demon remaining…" she said. "But you've lived your life of loneliness for five years already."

To Roger it felt ludicrous to be called strong by a demon of inhuman strength, but he could tell that her words were genuine. He remembered the times when he learned of being a Seeker. He remembered those feeling well he felt back then. But for Lili things were different. She was the only demon alive since a thousand years and furthermore she apparently held immortality. If he compared his situation with hers, his worries seemed to fade.

He didn't know what to answer. There wasn't anything he could say to make her situation any better. If he was in her situation, he wouldn't know what to do.

Roger was approaching the end of the field. He could gradually make out some houses through the crops.

"Lili," he said in a serious tone.

He turned around. She nodded.

There was no need for additional words.

Roger quietly proceeded towards the end of the field. Right at the end he peeked through the stalks. There were a few houses not worthy being called a village. If he had to guess, it would be the houses of the farmers that tended to these fields, but even though it was time for farmers to work, there wasn't any sign of life. They needed to cross the bridge behind the houses to get over the river.

He turned around to Lili, but she just shook her head. She didn't seem to hear any people, but they still had to be careful.

He pulled out the two black mantles from his bag and gave Lili hers. After putting them on, both of them slowly left the protection of the field and moved between the houses.

The window covers were closed and the doors as well. But there were barrels and sacks of crops at the walls that didn't make the impression of this place being abandoned.

Roger carefully proceeded between the houses, Lili close behind him.

"If anything happens, I promise to protect you," she whispered.

If anything, that made him feel more at ease, but still there was something about this place that made his body itch.

They continued further towards the wooden bridge.

There was only one house left they needed to pass. But then Lili shouted nervously from behind.

"Roger!"

It was the first time she had called his name, but his fluttery feelings didn't last long. Several doors smashed open and from each house a few knights came storming out. They were surrounded.

"Oh, cursed fate..." Roger mumbled to himself.

He stood back on back with Lili. Roger tried reaching for his knife but quickly was reminded of the state his shoulder was in.

He looked around for an escape, but there simply were too many of them. Especially at the back, the knights had gathered in rows. In each of the houses they had passed, a few knights had waited for them to come.

"Leave the back to me," Roger declared to Lili.

"Are you sure?!"

"I have a plan. It should work," he said, giving her a confident look. "I hope it does, at least."

Her face turned serious.

"I'll have trust in you then."

Roger took his knife in his left and ran towards a sack of crops leaning at a nearby house wall. The knights came charging at him. He quickly slid open the sack and grabbed its end, swinging it at the knights. The contents emptied out before him and created a half-moon from one wall to the other.

He reached for one of the oilskins he had bought in Spirithelm. The knights had almost reached him.

A shockwave went through his back as Lili awakened her demon powers. It was one of those time where he was glad that he had a demon on his side.

Roger had planned to delay the knights at the back and after Lili had dealt with the front, they could make a run for it, setting the bridge on fire after they had passed.

Roger concentrated on his part. He swiftly opened the skin and emptied its contents out in an arc on the crops. He quickly abandoned the empty skin and took his fire steel in his right hand. A piercing pain shot through his right shoulder, but he didn't stop. He grabbed the knife tightly with his left and readied the steel. He flashed over the metal with the sharp blade and several sparks flew towards the knights, eventually falling and hitting the ground.

The first was a miss. He tried another round of sparks. The knights were dangerously close by now. He prepared himself to run.

The sparks hit the ground. This time one of them hit the oil lake and a fiery flame shot up towards the sky, separating him and the horde of knights.

He turned around to run, but in that moment he heard an ear-piercing cry. It was not one of the knights. It was the voice of a girl in pain. It was Lili.

He looked at her in fear and saw her chest being pierced by a sword. Behind her stood the swordsman, grinning like the devil himself. Four knights, two on each side, fired a round of arrows at her. Her cries intensified.

The knight pulled out his sword and Lili dropped to the floor leaving a lake of blood that formed under her. Her head hit the ground and her voice gave in.

How could this have happened? He had seen her inhuman powers with his own eyes. Mere knights didn't stand a chance against her.

He remembered the similar scene that happened in

Prok, but somehow she seemed weaker. His body urged to help her, but he couldn't fight against the knights without a proper weapon. He only had a single knife that he had to wield with his weak arm. Roger impatiently was waiting for her wounds to recover.

The crossbowmen fired another round of arrows at her. She flinched up and let out another cry of pain. As her head hit the ground again and turned, he saw her face.

She looked at him, tears in her eyes that seemed to gradually lose their life. Something was wrong with her. Her wounds should have recovered by now.

The crossbowmen followed up with another round of arrows and the knight in the middle continuously stabbed her tiny body with his sword looking like he had gone insane.

Roger's chest felt tight. The heaviness of her fate rested upon him. She was immortal, right? She wouldn't die here? She was an immortal demon queen, right?

The knights continued wrecking her body. More and more wounds opened that added to the already gigantic blood lake beneath her.

He had to do something.

Behind him he heard the knights moving, and the flames were losing their strength.

He took another skin of oil and opened it. He took the open skin and bit hard on the leather, holding it with his teeth. With his fire steel and knife still in his hands he ran towards Lili and the knights.

Shortly before he reached them, he swung his head around, putting the force of his entire body into the motion and the oil splashed onto the knights' faces and armor.

They stumbled back a few steps and two of the crossbowmen dropped their weapons. He followed up with the fire steel, igniting a rain of sparks upon the knights.

He quickly turned his attention to Lili. He saw flames shooting up from the edge of his vision and heard the knights hitting the ground one after another, crying in pain.

Roger spit out the skin and looked at her. She was unconscious and her wounds were still open. Several arrows were stuck inside her. But there was no time to tend to her wounds. He decided to trust her words and believed she would open her eyes after they had escaped.

He picked her up. She had lost so much blood, she felt even lighter than before, but his shoulder was a nightmare to endure. He bit his teeth together and kept a steady hold, despite the pain.

He ran past the burning knights and headed for the bridge. But the knights from the back had caught up and blocked his path. He quickly made a turn to the left, having to run along the river. But there the knights were threatening to block his path as well.

He stopped.

He turned towards the river that was several feet below him. Its torrents were strong. He could tell. Any normal man that fell into the river would almost certainly drown.

The knights were closing in. He made up his mind. If he died, he would rather die saving someone, not in a ritual of death. He jumped.

Chapter 4

The next thing Roger felt was difficulty breathing. Water had made its way into his lungs. Roger's eyes went wide open and he had a coughing fit. Bit by bit the water made its way back up until finally everything seemed to have returned where it belonged.

Roger now realized that his surroundings had changed. Right in front of him was the same river he jumped into. He pulled his legs up that were still hanging halfway in the river's stream. On the other side was a thicket with trees leaning over the river's edge. He had stranded on a small patch of land where the river curved.

Various trees and greens were surrounding him. His clothes were heavy and drenched. He noticed parts of his bandage dangling down his arm.

He remembered the pain in his shoulder but endured it. Lili was more important. He looked around him and saw a black heart sticking out of a patch of grass near the river. He hastily crawled to the patch.

Lili was lying on her shoulder on a bed of grass painted in red. Countless arrows were sticking out from all angles. He opened the black, tattered mantle and looked at her. Her sword wounds had recovered, but from the arrows blood was leaking out still. He carefully took her upper body in his arm. Her mouth stood open, her eyes closed. But she was breathing shallowly at least.

He was glad that her words turned out to be true. She was an immortal demon. But the state she was in was not befit of one. Why did she lose to those knights? Why was she reduced to this sorry state, being tormented by those bastards?

Then her body suddenly flinched up and she started coughing out some water, the same he did.

She looked as drenched as her clothes, like every bit of energy had been sucked out of her.

"Are you fine?" he asked. But what was he saying? He could clearly see that she was far from it.

She untruly replied, "I am."

But the next moment she flinched again and her face tensed up.

"Could you pull them out?" she asked in a brittle voice. "I can't do it on my own."

"Are you sure? It's going to hurt," he replied, being fully aware that it had to be done.

She nodded.

Hesitantly he grasped an arrow that had pierced her lower leg. He gathered himself and with his eyes closed pulled it out forcefully. His insides turned when he felt the resistance of her flesh.

Lili cried out shortly, but quickly quieted down. When he opened his eyes again, he saw her covering her mouth with her hands to hold it in. The pain she had to endure was way more than any girl should have to endure. It was cruel. The knights were cruel. The world was.

He noticed he still held the arrow in his hand. The tip was covered in blood. He released his grip to throw it away but stopped when he noticed something. Faint steam emerged from the arrow's tip. It was coated with something else than her blood.

He had a realization, a strong guess. He looked around and found his bag lying close to the river.

"Wait a moment," he told her.

She gave him a confused look. Then he put her down, careful not break any of the arrows.

He went to his bag and opened it. Its contents weren't protected from the wet. The insides looked as sad as his bandage that was gradually unraveling.

He threw the arrow on the ground and pulled out his fire steel and knife. As he slid the knife over, but nothing happened, as he feared. A wet fire steel was as useless as no fire steel at all.

"Don't bother. There's no mistake," Lili spoke up in pain. "Holy water is the only substance that can do me this harm."

She had confirmed his thoughts. It was holy water. A secret substance originating from the church to fend of demonic monsters. Thinking about it, it wasn't a surprise that it worked on demons as well.

The knights from earlier came to his mind. He now realized that their armors did look different than the ones from the forest ambush. They were shinier.

Along with their swords and arrows, the armors must have been coated as well. If demons were this weak to it, it explained Lili's instant defeat.

He returned to her.

"The wound is gone," he said in surprise when he looked at her leg.

"Of course it is," she told him. "Just because I was struck with holy water, doesn't mean I lost my powers."

"Then, when I pull out all of them, you'll heal completely?"

"I will," she answered. "Now go ahead, I'm in pain."

He exchanged a look with her. While her face reflected the weak state she was in, he knew that she was strong. Far stronger than he'd ever be, but not because she was a demon or had powers no other demon had. She had lost everything and endured so much suffering but still accompanied him on his journey, showing him her smiles.

"Just bear with me," he said and then proceeded to pull the arrows out, one by one.

Each time he did, an awful shiver ran down his back. He could almost feel a part of her pain, and her admirable attempts at keeping herself from screaming didn't make him feel any better. But it had to be done, and so he did.

When the last arrow had been pulled, he removed the mantle from her and saw the final wound regenerate quickly before his eyes. Her body had recovered, but her clothes were still stained with blood and full of holes.

"How are you feeling?" he asked her carefully.

"You really want to know?" she said. "Awful. How else

could I feel? Any other would have just died on the spot and didn't have to endure this pain. Oh, how I envy them..."

Roger was relieved that she was already well enough to joke.

"I'll need a few hours to fully recover. And perhaps some food would aid in that!" she told him, showing a faint smile.

"Of course, I'll get something for you. I also want to know where we are exactly. I don't want to risk another unpleasant encounter."

"You don't want to stay in those, do you?" she asked, pointing at his drenched coat.

Luckily it was hot enough to go without. Roger turned around and rid himself of his coat and followed up with the rest of his clothes until the bare necessities.

Roger turned around again. He saw Lili struggling to remove her clothes as well. Her fingers grabbed onto her own coat but were too weak to hold on and slipped off.

Then she realized he was looking at her. In shock her eyes widened and two little tears appeared at the corners. She then quickly turned her head away, staring at the green next to her.

He deeply felt sorry for her. The attack had made her so weak that she couldn't even remove her clothes on her own.

Roger walked over to her and crouched down.

She slowly turned her head to take a glimpse of his face. Her cheeks had turned red and her lips shook in desperation.

"I'll help you."

Her mouth went wide. She tried breathing out some

words.

"N-no, thanks," she uttered. "I'll wait some time and do it myself."

She looked like she was ready to burst out in tears any moment. Her pride had been hurt a few times too often today. But he couldn't leave her like that.

"Your clothes are drenched and soaked with blood," he told her. "The sooner they're off the better."

"Ha!" she panted away from him. "Says the one who didn't hesitate to go bare chested in front of me."

He looked down on himself. Just some underwear was left that would dry quickly. She had told him to do something about his clothes and now she was complaining?

"I don't want you to catch a cold," Roger argued. "Or do demons even get ill?"

"They do," she admitted, still refusing to look at him.

"Then we better hurry," he said. "You didn't have any hesitations undressing yourself in the inn, remember?"

Her head moved a bit after he finished and then she lowered it. He must have hit a weak spot.

"It is pathetic for a demon to ask a human for help," she protested in shame.

"I understand that, but things are different now. We're traveling together and as you've helped me, I want to help as well."

She slowly turned her head and took a glance at him.

"Get it over with quickly then," she said, covering her face with both of her hands.

Roger had to smile. She being a demon queen with inhuman powers didn't matter. At this moment she was just a girl.

He went behind her back and noticed that the ribbons where still holding her hair as the night before. But since they were wet, he removed them first. Then he took the two ends of her coat.

"Can you move your arms backward for a moment," he asked. "Don't worry I can't see your face from here."

Slowly she removed her hands from her face and put them behind her back.

Roger carefully removed one sleeve after another and put the coat down beside her.

He then stood up and moved to her front. Her face was bright red. She looked at the ground beside her, eyes frozen.

Roger then proceeded and gently pulled her pants down.

He picked up her coat and the mantle as well and told her, "I'm done."

"I can see that," she muttered blushfully.

Roger then took both hers and his clothes to the river. He started with her coat and held it into the river's stream. The red slowly left the fabric and followed along the river.

When the coat was cleaned, he pulled it out of the water and looked at it. There were holes all over it. He felt a strong resentment against the knights that caused them in their aggression. He wouldn't forgive them even for a moment for what they did to her.

He drilled the coat to a spiral and wrung it out until most of the water had left.

Roger turned around with the coat and looked at Lili.

Lili had made herself comfortable in another patch of grass further away from the river. She hid herself behind her knees.

Then she noticed him.

"I hope you did not forget about the food you promised."

Roger went to a nearby tree and hung the coat on one of the branches.

"No, I didn't," he answered. "As soon as I'm finished here, I'll be looking."

Roger then proceeded with the rest of the clothes until all of them were hanging to dry.

"I'll be going then," he told her.

Lili sent him off with a face full of expectations and he started scouting the area.

Roger walked away from the river, making his way through the various plants that blocked his way.

After walking for a bit, the trees became sparser and a massive wall of stone came into his view. It was none other than the great walls of Strosa. They had come quite close to their next destination.

He carefully proceeded through the thicket to get closer to the walls. Then he crouched at the edge of the forest, hiding behind some bushes. He spotted a patch of forest that went further to the walls. From there the wall was only a sprint away.

He followed the thicket to his discovery and then took a closer look at the walls.

His view followed the stones upwards. There was not much of a chance to climb them. They were smoothed by the weather with no spots to place one's foot. At the top were watchtowers in regular intervals. He could spot a few small figures patrolling along the top from one tower to another. Leaving the cover of the forest was no option for him.

Roger didn't know the situation at the gates. He feared that they would thoroughly inspect any wagons that tried to enter. And posing as someone else was too risky. If the guards were equipped with holy water coated armor, Lili would have no chance and Roger never had one.

Flying wasn't an option either with so many guards patrolling the walls. Furthermore, he didn't know how high Lili could fly. Flying seemed to drain her stamina very quickly.

He noticed a ditch at the bottom of the wall that followed it along. He remembered something that he had heard a few years ago. Strosa was said to be one of the first cities to have a sewer system that removed excess rain and wastewater from the city. That way the city didn't suffer floods and could be built on top of a stone foundation. That made it impossible for enemy forces to enter by digging tunnels in case war broke out. Though this summer it would have been better to suck water from the outside, he thought.

Looking closer at the ditch, he couldn't see any water. From his angle he could just see the top portion, but there had to be water in it.

He looked around and set his sights on the highest tree in his surroundings and climbed up.

At the top he carefully removed the leaves in his way and looked down on the ditch. He now could see some water, just not that much. The heat must have claimed most of it. He could also see the exits of the sewer system that led into the ditch. Now that the water was only half the height, only a small portion of the sewer exits was covered.

But there were several iron bars blocking anyone from entering. They must have been at least as thick as a leg. Climbing the walls seemed easier than trying to pass those bars.

Maybe they had to try flying over the wall after all. If Lili could fly high enough, they wouldn't get seen if they were lucky. He decided to ask her when he returned.

He left the tree and jumped back down onto the forest ground.

When he took a step in the direction he came from, he was reminded loudly by his stomach that he promised to bring back food.

Eventually, he found some edible berries. He took a few of the giant leaves that were growing nearby and made a bag out of them. He picked berries until his improvised bag couldn't hold any more.

Then he headed back to Lili.

When he arrived at the place, Lili had moved from her patch of grass and was lurking over the river. Left to her a staple of fish were trashing around.

"Oh, you've returned!" she said, seemingly fully recovered.

"Did you not trust that I would bring food?" he asked her, remembering that he almost forgot.

"I did not doubt it once. Just those fish were asking to be caught. Boredom is a cruel disease."

"Then, how was it?" she followed up.

"Before that let's just eat. They shouldn't find us so soon."

Roger gathered some stray logs and made a fire in the

center of the place. Using small branches they pierced the fish and grilled them until brown. The sun prepared to set and the sky turned darker by the hour.

Lili was sitting across the fire on her patch and bit into the fish with relish. While chewing she said, "So?"

Her smacking words had a certain charm to it. He didn't feel like he had to tell her about human manners.

"The river brought us very close to the city walls," he began.

"Oh? That's fine, isn't it?"

"It is," he answered. "The knights won't find us so soon, but the problem arises how we get into the city. The walls are high and heavily patrolled."

"Hmm?" she summed, seemingly unconcerned, piercing another fish and holding it over the fire.

"There are exits of the sewer system in the ditch, but they are protected by heavy iron bars. So I thought that maybe you could fly high over the wall?"

She just looked at the fish, turning it every now and then.

"Of course I can, but that won't be necessary."

"What do you mean?"

"I can break those bars," she stated.

"They are as thick as a shoe."

"Be they as sturdy as diamond and as sizable as a horse, it doesn't concern myself."

Roger was once again surprised by the extent of her demonic powers. Imagining her breaking those massive bars was a huge contrast to herself a few hours ago.

"If that's possible, then I ask you to do just that."

"Certainly."

"We'll wait a few hours. The time when the sun has

set and the moon has yet to rise is the time we'll strike. The guards won't be able to see us in the dark."

After they had finished their feast, Roger put out the fire to avoid someone seeing the glow through the forest.

Lili had returned to her earlier pose hiding behind her knees and looking somehow unwell at the extinguished fire. It was getting harder to see every minute. They soon had to near the walls.

"Are you not feeling well?"

She lifted her heavy eyes.

"No, I was just thinking…"

"About your race?"

She forced a smile.

"It doesn't do me good if I get pitied by a human."

"It is no pity. I have my own things to worry about."

"You're right. You have many things to worry about because of me," she told him with guilt in her voice.

Roger didn't know what she was thinking about exactly, but it was true. There were many things that changed since he met her.

"There's nothing that can be done. Perhaps fate wanted it that way."

"You say, me getting defeated by mere humans was the will of fate? No! I refuse it! I failed you and it was my fault and my fault alone," she called furiously.

Roger was taken aback. He didn't expect her to be that angry at herself. He remembered when they were first ambushed. He had stopped her from killing the last knight. That man must have told the tale so that they could set another ambush at the bridge, being prepared with holy water. If this situation was anything, it would be his fault.

"Say, how did you manage to escape?" she asked. "You were injured and had a burden to carry."

"I set the knights that attacked you on fire," he began. "But I ended up having to jump into the river."

Her eyes widened for a second.

"And the knights at the back?"

Roger was a bit surprised. He thought that she had at least noticed the fire. He told her about the crops, the oil and the flame.

"Oh?" she said. "That's quite impressive."

"Did they use holy water coated weapons in the war also?"

"They did," she told him plainly. "Swords, arrows, spears... anything you can imagine."

"I see. But I never would have thought that they would coat their armor with holy water."

"You say their armors were coated?" she asked in surprise.

Roger paused for a moment of confusion.

"Wasn't that the reason you were defeated?"

"They had coated armor?" she murmured to herself, seemingly in shock.

Then her expression changed and her eyes wandered to the ground next to her, clenching her teeth together.

Was she angry? Roger couldn't tell from her eyes. It was getting hard to see their surroundings and her dark demon eyes were even harder to make out. But he realized that he shouldn't have brought up her defeat so casually. It must have hurt her pride once again.

Roger stood up.

"It's time. We need to go."

She quickly rose as well, brushing off the dirt from her clothes.

They started walking towards the wall.

It was a short walk and soon they arrived at the edge of the forest where Roger had climbed the tree before.

"Quite impressive," she said, looking at the walls.

"I think it's even more impressive if you can bend those bars," Roger answered, pointing in the direction of the sewer exit.

"Where? I can't see them."

"They are hidden in the ditch."

He went behind her and lifted her up with his hands under her shoulders. She was as light as ever. Surprisingly he could almost not feel his shoulder anymore.

"What do you think you're doing?" she asked, flabbergasted.

"I'm lifting you up."

"I can see that!" she said impulsively. "I'm asking you why."

She started waving with her arms and legs.

"I thought you could see the bars from there."

She calmed down for a moment and looked at the walls.

"I can see them, but only a small part of it," she said, almost sulkily.

"Do you not like being lifted?"

"It's not a matter of liking it," she said, now truly sulking. "It feels humiliating."

Roger couldn't hide his broad smile. It somehow felt awfully satisfying holding the last remaining demon queen like this.

She started struggling heavily with both her arms and legs.

"Let me down now. I cannot endure this any longer!"

Roger followed up on her wish and put her back on the ground.

She turned around angrily and gave him a look. He quickly hid his smile and raised his hands in front of him to fend off her stares.

"I'm sorry. I won't do it again," he told her. "Maybe," he added in his thoughts.

"If you truly understand..." she said, crossing her arms.

"So, do you think you can break them?"

Her face filled with a sinister smile.

"Who do you think I am?" she asked. "Unless they are holy water coated, of course."

Roger smiled.

"There are a lot of sewer exits. I doubt they could coat them so quickly."

"Then there's no problem."

Roger took the tattered mantle and held it in front of her. She gently took it and swung it around her. Roger did the same with his.

The sun had set, the moon had yet to rise. Darkness covered the area. Roger led the way to the ditch.

When he arrived, he looked down from the edge. It was a steep descent, but it was possible for them to slide down. But he had to be careful not to get his bag wet again, otherwise his fire steel would return to being dead weight.

"Can you swi—" he began, but the ditch quickly passed by and with a light unsettling he found himself directly next to the bars.

He looked at Lili whose eyes were quickly losing their red shine. He was taken aback and just stared at her. She showed him a sarcastic smile.

"Payback for earlier."

He let out a chuckle. Somehow their situation appeared way more enjoyable than it actually should.

She turned her attention to the bars. She couldn't grasp them fully even with both hands. They were truly massive.

He felt a light shockwave coming from Lili. Her eyes regained their red shine and her fangs ran down her lips. She had placed her tiny hands on two of the bars and started pulling them apart.

At first they did not butch, but after a few moments they slowly started giving in, changing their shape. At last they formed a gap sizable enough for a human to fit through.

She returned to her normal self. With the body of a small girl, she had managed to bend these massive bars to her will. Demons were not to be reckoned with.

"How was it?"

"Truly spectacular," he answered.

They looked each other in their half-serious faces. Then both of them burst out in laughter.

"This is hilarious," she said, holding her stomach. "I'm breaking into a human city with another human that is feared more than a real demon."

"I can be quite scary," Roger claimed, smiling. "But let's go before the moon rises too high."

He took the first step through bars and Lili followed after him. There was no light in the sewers which was to be expected since they normally were flooded.

They were walking in shallow waters. Roger's shoes were soaking wet. After just a few steps, they stood in utter darkness.

"Can demons see in the dark?" he asked.

"No, but remember, we have good ears."

"Sadly, that doesn't help us navigate through here," he sighed.

"Don't take demon ears for too little!" she told him. "I can navigate through here just fine with just my hearing. Your voice reflects countless times from these stony walls. I can tell the shape."

Roger was surprised. He didn't know that hearing could be used this way.

"Perhaps I did take demon ears for too little," he admitted even though he thought they already were quite impressive. "Then, can you tell where there's an exit?"

"Hmm… there does seem to be a branch ahead."

When they arrived at the branch, Roger noticed that indeed the sound of their voices had changed.

"So, which direction now?" he asked.

"This way."

Roger paused for a moment.

"I can't tell where you're pointing in the dark."

It followed a moment of silence. Then he felt her grabbing onto his coat and pulling to the right.

"This way," she said again, slightly embarrassed.

Roger silently followed her lead until she stopped.

"What's wrong?"

"We're here. The top leads outside."

Roger raised his head. And indeed he could see some

bright spots of light coming through the cover.

"Where's the ladder?"

"There is none," she answered plainly.

Roger took a few moments to comprehend her words.

"You mean there's no way up?!"

Roger hadn't thought of the possibility that there was no way to leave the sewers from the inside. He had expected a ladder at each exit in case the city checked the sewers for necessary repairs or other issues.

"Not for humans, at least," she answered.

He remembered that he had a demon with him.

"You're saying you can fly to the top?"

"It's too cramped in here. I can't fly," she answered. "But I can jump."

"Demons can't just fly, they can jump high as well?"

"Our powers give us superior physical strength to humans. That's all there is to it. If humans can jump, demons can jump higher. If human can run, demons can run faster. That's how it works."

"Demons are surprisingly similar to humans," he realized.

"Just that demons have tails and wings, dark hair and eyes, live far longer and can change into their demon form, they are both very similar," she said sarcastically.

Roger could tell that she didn't like being compared to humans.

"A great demon as yourself can surely bring us out of here," he suggested, returning her sarcasm.

"My great presence indeed can do such as thing, but there's a risked involved," she told him. "There is nothing to grab onto. I'd have to jump and lift the cover and then grab onto the edge. But there are no hands free to keep the cover from falling onto the ground and making some noise."

That was indeed a problem. If the cover were to hit the ground, it would undoubtedly wake someone. But there wasn't much of an alternative.

"Can you hear if there is anyone up there?"

"The sewers are keeping the sounds to themselves, but I can assure you that at least there's nobody above the cover."

"Then you jump and grab onto the edge while I lift the cover."

"A plan indeed, but the mantles are in the way."

"Oh… sure. Let's leave them off for a moment."

While storing the mantles inside his bag, another pressing question came to his mind.

"Wait. Do we even fit through at the same time?"

Roger had noticed that the cover didn't seem particularly wide.

"I'm not that big. If you fit through, I do as well," she said, brushing off his worries with ease.

Roger was a bit uncertain after hearing her vague reasoning, but he had to trust her on that matter.

He could hear her walking to his front and then she hugged him tightly around his waist.

"What are you doing?"

"I'm holding on to you."

"I can see—"

Roger realized that they had a similar conversation before, but their roles were reversed.

"I'm going to jump. Are you prepared?"

Roger quickly pulled his arms up.

"I am."

Then suddenly she jumped.

In the blink of an eye the cover touched his fingers. It pushed his arms back quite a bit before he could resist its force. Then the bright moonlight entered his eyes.

After a moment he could make out a street leading to a dead end along the wall that was just meters away. They had managed to come to the other side.

Then Roger started falling down causing panic for a moment, but his armpits were caught by Lili's tiny arms that she used to hold onto the street behind his back. It was one of those times where he could see Lili's red glowing demon eyes up close. There was something about them that drew him in.

However, something else caught his attention. He couldn't feel the cover in his hands anymore. He looked up and saw it spinning in the air. It was falling down, threatening to hit the stony streets with an ear-shattering sound. He reached out with his arms and managed to hold onto it, but its weight pulled them down. With just a tiny sound, the cover touched the ground. Roger had managed to absorb most of its force.

He let out a huge sigh.

Then Roger heard a muffled voice.

"I can't breath…"

He quickly realized that he had leaned over Lili to catch the cover. Her face was tightly buried in his coat. He carefully placed the cover on the street and leaned backwards.

"I'm sorry," he whispered.

He looked at her slightly angry face. Now not only her eyes were glowing red, her nose also was. Contrary to what he should be thinking, it actually looked quite amusing. He turned his face to the side to avoid showing her that thought on his face.

When he did, he noticed a door that led into the wall. Light shone through the gaps in the wood.

"We have to get away from here," he told her quietly.

Roger climbed up and exited to his back. His bag was making things a bit complicated but eventually he was sitting on top of the street together with his bag.

Lili followed shortly after him and he carefully put the cover back in its place.

He further observed his environment. The wall was to his left, and to his front and his right were walls of other buildings. He turned around. This was the only way out.

However, there seemed to be someone inside the wall. Roger quietly sneaked along the wall getting closer to the door.

"There it is again, my friend. Checkmate! That's what they call it!" a man with a heavy voice shouted laughingly.

"How could this have happened? Again?! Impossible!" another man lamented in despair.

Then Roger heard a door smashing open and someone else entered the room.

"What are you doing here?" he shouted angrily. "This is not a tavern for your amusement. You are to catch a Seeker and a demon, not sitting around playing chess!"

Roger realized the danger.

He quietly pulled out their two mantles and they put them back on. He carefully took a glance through the keyhole.

There were two guards sitting at a wooden table with a set of chess on top of it. A third, rather thickly man who appeared to be of higher rank filled the door leading further into the wall.

The two men hurriedly cleaned up the table and then stood up synchronously.

"Yes, Sir!" they echoed.

"I don't want to see that sight again," the thickly man told the guards and turned around exiting the room.

They had to get away before the guards resumed their work.

Roger gave Lili a signal and they quickly flashed by the door.

He wanted to get as close to the port as possible before the day came. The sea was to the west and that was where they were heading.

There weren't any people around and guards weren't patrolling around either. It seemed the city had underestimated them, thinking that they would enter through the gates.

Eventually, after quite some time, Roger could see the sea in the distance. They had arrived at the port, but there were no people around.

He needed to ask someone for when the next ship to Crystalreach departed, but it seemed that matter had to wait until the morning.

After looking around for a bit, Roger spotted a stable in a side alley leading away from the port. He stopped there and pulled out his skeleton keys and took care of the lock.

"Say, why do you have keys for all the locks we encounter?" Lili asked suddenly.

"I don't have keys for all the locks. It's just that these keys can open those types of locks, warded locks as they call them. They are cheap to craft but lack security."

He showed one of the keys to her.

"It's just like a normal key but with only the essential parts. A warded lock blocks any key that doesn't have the right shape, but if you get rid of the shapes altogether, you have a skeleton key like this."

Roger wasn't sure if Lili had understood him or if she was silently impressed, but she didn't answer.

He just continued opening the lock and then finally both of them moved inside the stable. Naturally, there were horses inside but also a haystack that would serve them for the night.

"Say, can you bind my hair again?" she asked.

Roger had just closed the door and turned around.

"I guess I can do that," he answered. "Any ideas?"

"I'll leave that up to you." she said happily, turning around.

Roger took out the two ribbons from his bag and went behind her. He had a feeling that he could try something more challenging this time.

He again halved her hair at the neck level, but this time he pulled it up to the side and added some hair from the front. He took the ribbon and made a loop around the tail. He did the same thing for the other side and reviewed his work.

It did indeed look like it challenged something, but perhaps not his skills.

"Are you done?" she asked after some while.

"I guess I am."

She again followed the usual routine spinning around a few times and then showed him a satisfied smile.

This time he had feared she wouldn't like it, but it

seemed his worries were unnecessary.

Roger then neared the haystack and lay down.

"I'm sorry it's not a very fitting place for a queen."

She also lay down behind him and answered.

"I have no right to be called a queen. I've lost my race and if it weren't for my immortality, I would have died long ago."

When he turned around to answer, he saw her having fallen asleep already. He turned back and did the same.

Roger opened his eyes. The gentle glow of the rising sun came through the gaps in the wooden gate. He turned around and shook Lili on her shoulder.

"Wake up," he said. "We need to leave."

She slowly struggled her eyes open and looked at him with a sleepy face. When she rose her upper body, there was still a piece of straw sticking to her cheek. Her hair also was a mess being full of those.

"You awake?"

Her eyes gradually returned to their normal size. "Certainly."

Roger stood up, removing the piece of straw on her cheek and headed to the door.

He slowly opened it and took a peek outside. He could see the light at the horizon that had been born. The port was filled with a faint mist.

He turned around to check on Lili. She looked at him with a wide mouth and somehow faintly red face. It must have been the morning shine.

"What's wrong?" he asked, startling her.

"Nothing," she said hastily and looked to the side.

"Then let's go."

"Certainly."

Both of them moved outside the stable into the silent city and Roger clicked the lock back in place.

"Some port workers must be working already. I'll ask them about the ship. Just wait here until I return."

She gave him a quick nod and Roger left the alley.

He pulled the hood of his mantle over his head.

In the distance he spotted a bunch of workers carrying goods from a ship. It must have arrived during the night.

He walked to them.

"Excuse me," Roger spoke to one of the workers. "Do you know when the ship to Crystalreach will depart?"

The man turned around. He seemed to be the overseer since he was just standing there, watching the others work.

His arms were crossed and Roger couldn't read his mood. A brown mustache was floating over his lips and his expression could be only described as sturdy.

Then he opened his mouth.

"Crystalreach, you say? It should arrive tonight and depart the morning after," he stated without showing any emotions.

Roger gave him his thanks and turned around to head back to the stable.

"How was it?" Lili greeted him on his return.

"The ship will depart tomorrow."

"One day..." she said, almost complaining.

"It could have been much longer. We are lucky it's so soon."

"But it means we need to stay unseen in this city for another day."

"We managed for more days then one, we'll manage another," Roger told her.

"Perhaps that's true." Her expression had cleared up.

"For now let's just get away from the port. It's going to get crowded here."

Roger started walking into the side alley and Lili followed right next to him.

Eventually, the city became livelier. Even far away from the main street in the lonely alleys between the houses, they could hear the voices of stand owners shouting and citizens talking. The only noise that was louder was a growling next to Roger.

"You're hungry?"

"No, I'm just pretending."

"Then perhaps we don't need any food."

In truth, Roger wanted to avoid buying food at all costs, but he knew the time would come where even he would get hungry. And unlike her, he couldn't survive without food, especially not when they were sailing for a long time.

He noticed an evil glare coming from his side.

"Sure, sure, I'll buy you something," Roger said in an attempt to sooth her. A successful attempt.

They headed closer to the main street and Roger pulled his hood over once again. He told Lili to wait and then entered the crowded main street.

He was relieved that he wasn't the only one that had such a shady outfit. And in truth there were some travelers who preferred to have their face hidden.

Roger walked up to the next stand that sold some bread and ordered three loafs. He needed to make preparations for the coming days.

After he had paid he returned to Lili and put one loaf in her hands. She heartily pressed her fangs into it and ripped off a far too large piece.

He watched her fighting with the bread. Eventually, her fangs gained superiority and the piece slowly vanished inside.

When she had swallowed, she gave Roger a look. He quickly turned his gaze away and bit into his own, being a bit more reserved.

After a cracking sensation, he noticed that the bread had to be at least a couple of days old. For a moment he feared that the cracking came from his teeth but was pleasantly surprised when he chewed through the rest. The remaining piece and the other loaf he stored inside his bag. He wasn't in the mood of fighting through another bite.

Then they continued walking further from the main street again.

"Isn't it good that your next spell is in another realm?" she spoke up. "Imagine it being somewhere in the city."

Truly that thought had crossed Roger's mind. After being discovered as a Seeker, he would have a very hard time if the spell was in the same territory or even human realm still.

"I guess it is, but the elven realm is not to be taken lightly."

In truth it was precisely the unknown that made him respect the realm.

"You're right. There's the bows after all…"

"Do they use coatings as well?" Roger asked, realizing that Lili should know a thing or two about the elves.

"They do. More so than any other races. Not only holy water but extract from poisonous or paralyzing plants and many other hellish things," she told him, shivering.

"Do those coatings affect demons as well?"

"Certainly. Many of my race have fallen to them."

"And what about you?" he asked. After all, she was immortal.

"Poison won't kill me, but I'll feel the effects for some time and other coatings work as well, just that they don't kill me."

Roger decided to refrain from asking whether she had any personal experience. He could hurt her pride again.

"And you made it sound so good that we can escape from here," he said, half-serious.

"Better sneaking through the elven realm than running from a horde of coated knights."

"That might be true."

After some while Lili stopped and when Roger turned to look at her, he was painfully reminded of the reason.

He had once again failed to bind the ribbons properly. One of her tails had collapsed.

Lili picked up the ribbon that had left her hair in favor of the ground and turned around with a suggesting smile.

Roger's hand met his forehead.

"Should I rebind them?" he asked, frustrated.

"I feel like going without for now would bring in some variation," she said. "Can you remove the other one... before it removes itself?"

Defeated, Roger went to her and untied the remaining ribbon. He regretted now not having someone teach him during the time he lived in Brineguard.

"Here you go," he said, holding the untied ribbon in his hand.

Her hair was now the same he knew from when he first met her.

Lili gave him the other one and Roger stored them inside his bag.

She smiled at him.

"Then, let's go," she said happily.

Both continued walking through the shadows between the houses.

Lili walked in front of him with her hands intertwined at the back, her hair waving with every one of her gentle steps.

Suddenly, she stopped.

"There's something I have to tell you," Lili then said. "Someone behind us left the crowd and is heading for us."

Roger felt a shock running through his body. Have they been discovered?

"Let's change course then. Maybe it's just a coincidence," he said and turned at the next corner.

"He's gone now," she said after a while.

Roger felt a sense of relief. The sun had risen to the top and there was still more than half a day they needed to get by unseen.

But now that they had changed their course, they were getting closer to the main street.

Then Roger's eyes caught something on the wall and his legs froze.

Blood left his face as he stared at the piece of paper hanging on the wall. It showed a sketch that resembled him closely. Next to it was his companion with her wings spread out. Below the words "Seeker - Demon WANTED Report on sight." appeared.

Roger realized that this couldn't be the only poster hanging in the city. The port worker had seen his face. He couldn't tell whether he knew of his identity right from the beginning, but if he encountered one of the posters after, he'd report him immediately.

Roger hastily ripped the poster from the wall and rumpled it in his bag.

"What's wrong?" Lili asked, turning around.

"Nothing, but we're getting too close to the main street," he said, grabbing her hand and leading the way away from the main street.

"Ha? There's obviously something wrong. Why aren't you telling me?"

Roger just ignored her and sped up his pace.

"I'm asking you what's wrong, I say," she pressed further, her voice containing a slight anger.

"Why don't you answer me? Hey! Roger!" she shouted, now being fully angered.

"It's nothing. We just need to get away from here," he shouted back, agitated.

"Wha—" he heard and then Lili suddenly stopped.

He turned around and saw the reason. She was staring at another poster on the wall showing both of them clearly above the threatening words.

He suddenly was overcome by immense guilt. Not only did he try to hide this from her, he also was the reason why those posters were hanging in the first place. If he hadn't stopped her from killing the last knight that escaped from the ambush in the forest, they couldn't have set up another ambush with holy water so soon. It was all his fault.

"Be quiet," she said. But there was no sense of anger in her voice anymore.

She closed her eyes.

"We are truly being chased. There are others coming after us. I hear their jangling armor," she told him, pointing at the direction of the port.

"We need to hurry," she said.

Roger didn't know what to say. She wasn't angry with him even though this situation was his doing.

"What's wrong?" she then asked. "We need to hurry."

"We do," went over his lips and his legs set into motion.

They were hurrying through the alleys with large steps. Neither said a word.

After a while, Lili spoke up again.

"They've started moving faster," she told him.

Her words made pearls of sweat drip from his hair.

"How close are they?" he asked nervously.

"Close."

Roger and Lili started running. But after another while, Lili spoke up again.

"They are moving in from the main street. They are starting to surround us from one side."

They further increased their speed. Corner after corner shot by Roger's eyes. They made a turn here, a turn there in an attempt to shake off their chasers.

But then they had moved close to the main street again. The next corner they passed, Roger saw some knights in shiny armor entering from the main street. Both his face and theirs widened in shock.

"They're here!" Roger heard one of them shouting after he vanished behind the next corner.

"Lili," he shouted, panting. "Is there any way we can go?"

"Follow me," she said. "I can't hear anyone from there."

Roger followed her turn after turn until they entered a wide plaza far away from the main street. The sun that filled the place blended him for a moment. Both him and Lili had stopped.

In front of him was a platform made of stone. On top of it was a wooden structure with a sling dangling down from it. And he saw a man he recognized. Around him was an arc of countless crossbowmen pointing their weapons at them and swordsmen to their side. The sun danced on their armor pieces.

"Well, well," the man raised his voice. "So we meet again, Persefall."

Anger built up inside him. It was the same man that he had met on his way to Spirithelm, the man that had used his nobility to rob him of his herbs. It was the viscount of Strosa, Lewis Gaynesford.

"Who would have thought that you were the Seeker," he chuckled arrogantly. "I have to thank you for your herbs the other day. They were splendid indeed, fetched a high price for me. If you still have yours, perhaps you could hand them over? Would be a waste if they were stained with blood," he said with an evil smile.

"You used your nobility to rob me! You're a disgrace to all honest people," Roger unleashed his anger.

"Bold words, Persefall! But make no mistake. You're a Seeker, don't forget. Who could be a greater disgrace than a filthy Seeker?" he spit out with aggression.

"Persefall! You'll soon be wishing that you were hung right here," he added, showing his teeth.

"THAT'S ENOUGH!" Lili shouted suddenly. "This man taught me that not all humans are contemptible. But you! You are one of those that should have perished in the war!"

Roger could feel the force in her voice.

"Oh? So you're the demon the rumors told. Why aren't you dead? Shouldn't you be the one that perished in the war? Did you hide in a corner in fear for a thousand years, leaving your race to die? How honorable!"

Roger felt a shockwave coming from Lili and he saw the viscount stumbling back a few steps. But Lili stopped after hearing the clattering of armor from the crossbowmen that readied their weapons. She seemed to be genuinely afraid.

"Woa woa! I've heard what you did to my men. You seem to be quite dangerous. But I've also heard holy water reduced you to a state as helpless as a baby!"

The viscount quickly took back his place and raised his arm.

Then things happened too quickly for Roger to follow. He took a glimpse of Lili that kicked a few wooden crates past him that had stood at the corner.

He felt the air of the crates flashing past and heard some moans shortly after. When he turned his head, he spotted some knights behind him that had collapsed under the crates. She had made a pathway for their escape, Roger realized.

"FIRE," the viscount shouted, making Roger's head turn back to his front.

Lili stood before him, facing him. Her wings grew large in an instant. Lili's face captured his entire being.

Then Roger heard countless pierces in just a single moment. She coughed up blood. Her face grew weaker, but she kept standing.

Roger realized what had happened. She had shielded him from the arrow fire. But those arrows were coated.

"I'm sorry," she said in a weak voice. "I've destroyed your quiet life."

She looked him in the eyes. Then she coughed up blood again.

Tears started forming in her face as she looked at him.

"I know I can't make up for it," she continued. "But I can at least protect you at the end, like you protected me."

Tears started rolling down her cheeks.

"Roger," she continued, crying. "This is where we part. Please. Escape from here and continue your travels in the elven realm."

Roger couldn't breathe. He couldn't move nor form any word.

Her eyes flooded and another few tears ran down her cheeks. She formed a weak smile with her tiny mouth.

"I'm glad it was you who unsealed me!"

The world seemed to stop for a moment and her words echoed through his mind.

Those were her final words.

When time started working again, countless swords pierced her body from behind. Her blood splattered onto his face. He saw her losing all of her strength, her body only being held up by the swords.

He stumbled backwards a few steps. A sea of blood

formed under her. Then his legs moved on their own and he started running. It wasn't him. It was the Seeker inside him that made him run. If he were just a normal man, he would have frozen on the spot, unable to move.

He passed the knights under the crates and escaped through the pathway she created. He ran just as she told him and passed the main street, storming through the crowd to the other side. He kept running. He ran as he never had done in his entire life.

Chapter 5

It was a long night, a night of running, struggling to escape the chasing knights.

Roger supported himself with one hand on the cold stone wall and sunk down on his bottom, leaning against the wall.

He had managed to shake off his chasers. His legs were tired. He was tired. He had sat down in a side alley near the port. That was where he would board the ship in time. It was still dark, but the morning was nearing.

Roger thought about what happened. About Lili, about the knights, about his life as a Seeker. It all began that night in Spirithelm when he conducted his deciphering ritual. Of all the spells he had seen, this was the strangest.

He had unsealed a sleeping demon queen. The queen of a race that was exterminated a thousand years ago. And he carried her out of church after she had collapsed from shock. Perhaps if he had abandoned her, all of this would have never happened.

He then later learned of her identity and she somehow accompanied him on his lonely journey. Perhaps he had wished for someone to share his loneliness.

In Prok he then learned that they were being chased and were found out the same night. From that time on he was living a life of hiding, a life that was constantly at threat.

They somehow managed to escape from Prok and he learned of the next spell's location. They were ambushed two times on their way to Strosa and both suffered injuries.

And then yesterday happened. Lili was caught. She told him to run, that she caused him trouble.

It was true. Since she appeared, he had nothing but trouble. If he didn't meet her, he would have quietly traveled through the cities and boarded the ship on the same day. But he wouldn't have been chased. He wouldn't have to fear for his life. He wouldn't have felt the pressure that if he made one mistake, he'd be dead.

Even though his life was the cursed life of a Seeker, he still wanted to live, to see the world, and perhaps, he'd find the Seeker's Dream and could settle down somewhere, making friends and light chatter.

He could only hope that the spell after the next wouldn't lead him back to the human realm. After a few years perhaps, people would have forgotten about him and he could return. Then everything would have returned to normal.

Perhaps this was how it should be. This was the life fit

for a Seeker.

Roger turned his head and looked at the horizon. He spotted a dark spot in the distance. He just could make out the pointy sails at the top. It was the ship that would bring him to Crystalreach. It would dock this night and depart in the morning. Then he would be on his way to his next ancient spell.

The elven realm was a new experience for him. In his entire five years as a Seeker, this was the first time he had to leave the realm.

He had left his home territory before, but crossing the sea was an entirely different situation. He was unsure about what was awaiting him. The only thing he knew was that elves had isolated them from the other races of their own will.

He wondered what they would do if they discovered that a human had entered their realm. Would they welcome him as a rare guest? Or would they try to kill him? Those were questions that he could only answer in time.

He also didn't know how Seeker's were regarded in their realm. It was unlikely that they'd welcome a Seeker even of their own race, but as they were mysterious, the answer might be mystifying as well.

At least one thing he knew for sure. He would enter the realm as an unknown man. He wouldn't be chased if he kept himself hidden. There would be no knights that lusted for his throat. His next spell's location was perhaps the most convenient of all choices.

Roger watched the ship at the horizon becoming bigger and bigger until he could see it in his full brilliance, docking at the port.

He watched the crew lowering the sails and preparing to dock. They were running on deck as chaotic as a gathering of flies on the remnants of rotten food.

He watched them unload the cargo with dark eyes. It took a while before the last box had been unloaded and the crew left the ship, eagerly walking into the city. They were laughing and joking and were visibly looking forward to their beer in the tavern that soon opened.

Finally, it was time. Now was Roger's chance to board the ship unseen.

He opened his bag and pulled out his black mantle. For a moment he wondered where the second, tattered mantle was but quickly remembered.

He rose slowly and put the mantle on. He noticed some red spots on it and quickly focused his view elsewhere.

His legs were shaking, probably from all the running. It had been an exhausting night for him, a night he didn't wish to repeat. He was lucky enough that he had enough stamina to outrun a horde of knights, but with their heavy armors things were in his favor.

His view was focused on the ship. He carefully looked around him, checking for any people nearby and then he started walking.

But one step was the furthest he came. He tripped and his legs gave in.

In the blink of an eye he found himself on all fours, the contents of his bags scattered to his side.

Lifelessly he made his bag stand and returned one thing after the other. Two skins, one filled with oil, the other with water, one and a half loaves of bread, his fire steel, skeleton keys and...

He hesitated as he picked up the next thing.

He looked at it. Suddenly he couldn't see it clearly anymore. His vision became blurry. He blinked. It was a brush. A hair brush that he had forgotten about. One that was not intended for his hair that was hardly long enough to make use of it. It was the brush he had bought for Lili as a present the day they were found out.

Wet drops hit they cold ground as he looked at it.

"Lili... Lili..." he mumbled.

His tears came out in streams and he remembered her face the last time he saw her.

"I'm glad it was you who unsealed me," she had said.

Roger was overcome with grieve and his emotions were taking over. He stemmed his hands on the ground to keep him from falling over, the brush still in one of his hands. The ground darkened bit by bit like from a downpour.

Roger cried alone in the darkness of the night. There was nobody that heard him. He was alone with his grieve. There was nobody that understood him. His heart felt painfully empty. There was something missing, someone. A small girl that was not a deadly manslaughterer, but a kind and suffering demon queen that had the noble wish of resurrecting her race. But she wasn't there, next to him. She was far away, in the hands of the viscount, Lewis Gaynesford, a man who could truly be called a demon.

Roger made up his mind. He wouldn't leave without her. Before he knew it she had become a welcomed part of his life. She freed him from his curse of loneliness and he wanted her to be here by his side.

He returned the brush and the remaining things to

his bag and stood up, determined, his sight set on just one goal. He noticed that his legs were no longer shaking.

At this moment he felt powerful, ready to do anything to get her back.

He started running through the side alleys, one corner after another. Roger's legs carried him through the city maze, having one destination. It was a grand structure with lots of banners flattering in the wind on top. It belonged to the ruler of the city, the viscount, Lewis Gaynesford. That's where he and Lili would be.

Between the houses most of the moonlight didn't reach the ground. It was dark, but Roger had no trouble navigating through. It was as if his eyes were illuminating the way. All he heard were his footsteps as he moved through the quiet night.

And at last he had reached the viscount's fort. He carefully looked around the corner.

It was a vast place before the property and the building itself stood like a tower. The fort was surrounded by a rich garden protected by iron fences. The top of those were razor sharp spears that would discourage even the most eager thief.

Just one gate led into the property. Two torches were lighting it up in the dark. In front of it were two knights that blocked the way.

He could see the torchlight reflecting on their armor. It had the same familiar shine of coating. Both held a long spear in their hand, resting it on the ground. The metal tips sharply glistened in the torch shine. He couldn't tell if they were also coated, but that was of no concern to him.

Roger opened his bag and checked that everything was in place. He took his fire steel and knife in his hands and hid them under his mantle. Then he left the alley and walked towards the knights.

His steps echoed through the place. He had lowered his face and pulled his hood far over so that they wouldn't recognize him immediately. He saw the knights' legs reacting to his nearing.

"Hey! Reveal yourself at once!" one of the knights shouted.

But Roger ignored him.

He saw them ready their spears, lifting them from the ground.

"Don't come any further or we'll attack you," they said, but Roger continued to approach unchanged.

The knights were hesitating. Roger was the opposite. He lifted his head and looked them in the eyes. The soft torchlight shone on his skin and their faces dropped. They looked like they were fearing him. They tumbled backwards a few steps.

"It's him," one of the mumbled. "It's the Seeker."

Then their expressions changed. It was if they were overcome with hatred. Their hands tensed up tightly around the spears and they started charging at Roger.

He had waited for this moment. His hands left his mantle and he pointed the fire steel at the knight on the left.

He forced the knife over it, creating a spectacle of sparks flying at the knight. Once they had hit, the armor burst up in flames.

The other knight stopped in shock, looking at the

other, but Roger quickly pointed the fire steel at him and ignited another wave of sparks. The sparks reached the other armor and it as well burst up in flames. Both of them fell on the ground, screaming and winding.

Holy water coated armor was a double sided blade. While it effectively rendered demons useless once they touched it, it was also highly combustible. Like the hell they imagined demons to come from, they were now suffering in their own.

The pathway into the property was open. Roger ran into the garden with full speed. The entrance to the tower was straight ahead, so he took course towards it. But the screams of the knights had alarmed another two that came storming out of it. Their faces were in staggering realization.

Then they quickly readied their swords and charged at Roger. He took his fire steel in turn, readying the knife to dance over the steel. He slid it over before the first knight reached him. The sparks hit his armor.

Roger's eyes widened. The knight's armor didn't ignite. He noticed that it lacked the shine of the others.

The knight charged through the wave of sparks and swung his sword at Roger. He stepped backwards in reflex, but his realization was too late. The sword tore through his clothes and he felt a slicing pain on his chest.

He fell backwards. But the knight didn't stop and the other one followed right after him. Roger evaded the next sword swing and started running.

He checked his chest with his hand. His clothes soaked up the blood and his hand returned bloody as well. But he could breath normally, just that he felt the pain with each breath. The sword didn't cut deep.

Roger continued running.

He spotted a bed of freshly seeded plants. He pulled his hood back and looked over his shoulder at the knights.

They couldn't keep up with his speed, so he lowered his to have them catch up. When he arrived at the bed, he quickly crouched down and took a handfull of dirt.

With a swift turn he smashed the dirt into the first knight's face, robbing him of his eyesight. The knight came to a stop, letting go of his sword. Roger quickly took his last skin of oil and followed up with a splash into the knight's face.

The other knight, surprised by the sudden halt, crashed into the first making him fall to the ground face down.

The other, now even more angered than before, quickly gathered himself after the impact and continued to charge at Roger.

Roger continued running further into the garden searching for an opportunity.

When he had circled the tower to the back, he spotted a sizable pond with plants neatly placed around it. He stopped at the shore and turned around, waiting for the second knight.

When the knight was close enough, Roger quickly pulled his fire steel from under his mantle and blinded the knight with its sparks. The knight hesitated for a moment and gave Roger the time he needed.

He quickly circled the knight until he stood behind him. Then he jumped at the knight with his feet leading the front. He used his hands to push himself off the ground giving his kick more force. His legs hit the hard armor, sending the knight flying into the pond.

Roger looked at him struggling with his hands. The darkness of the pond showed its deepness. The knight was dragged down into the water slowly while more and more air under his armor escaped to the surface. His heavy armor would be the end of him.

The first knight suddenly screamed from the distance.

He had recovered and was now drawing closer with his sword pointed at Roger's throat. Roger turned around and ignited another set of sparks when the knight entered his range.

The remaining oil on the knight's face caught fire in an instant and he suffered a similar fate as the knights at the gate.

Roger circled back around the tower until he reached the entrance. No reinforcements were present. The viscount had underestimated him.

He entered.

The tower stood on massive stone walls that would even challenge other territories if they were to invade.

The floor quickly turned into a red carpet. Roger followed it.

Torches were lit, hanging on the walls in regular intervals. Majestic paintings of the previous viscounts presented themselves proudly on the walls.

He arrived at a staircase leading up and down.

The carpet led the way to the top, the uncarpeted stairs down to the cellars.

Roger went down to the cellars. He walked the cold and unforgiving stairs until his path was blocked by a metal door.

It had a small barred window at the top. Through it

he could make out the insides. He saw dozens of bars that separated countless cells and at the end, there was another metal door tightly sealed with a lock and a massive metal bar.

That had to be where Lili was.

Roger's gaze went down to the lock. It was an unfamiliar sight. It was not a simple warded lock that he could open with his skeleton keys.

He pulled and pushed the door back and forth in hope someone had forgotten to lock it, but his attempts remained futile.

Roger had to get the keys to get into the cellar to free Lili. And there was only one person that could have the keys in this tower.

He quietly walked the stairs back up and further climbed to the upper floors.

At the floor above, there was just one door and the continuing stairs that awaited him.

The carpet went further up the stairs. Roger concluded that the carpet would lead him to the viscount, but he couldn't ignore any remaining knights in the tower. If he went up to the viscount and some knights cornered him from below, he would have no way out.

He quietly neared the door on this floor. It was mostly wooden, but had metal plates worked into it, making it quite sturdy.

Carefully, he pressed his ear against the door.

"…really got you," a male voice said inside.

"Don't screw with me!" another voice shouted aggressively. "When he is caught, I'll personally conduct the ritual on him. He'll be regretting that he did this to my face. He'll be wishing that he died right there at the bridge."

"But you got the back at the demon, didn't you? Not many can boast about stabbing a demon with their sword," the first man encountered.

"Oh, I'll be sure to teach that demon another lesson," the second man declared wildly. "I already made sure she knows her place. Humans have won the war. Demons have no business in this world. For all I care she can suffer down there for eternity until her mind breaks."

"I'll be looking forward to partake in this lesson as well," the first man said. "Let's ask the viscount, right now. I'm sure your burned face itches you to."

Roger heard one of them pushing a chair back, followed by footsteps closing in.

He had no doubts. One of the men inside was the knight that had pierced Lili's tiny body with his sword relentlessly at the bridge. He had survived the fire.

The footsteps doubled and neared. Roger quickly pulled out his bundle of skeleton keys, searching for the right one. When he found it, he inserted it into the keyhole and turned.

A loud click echoed through the floor. A short moment of silence followed.

Then Roger flinched as one of the trapped men inside threw himself at the door.

"Hey?! Who's there?!" he shouted aggressively. "Unlock the door at once!"

It was the voice of the knight with the burned face.

Roger didn't answer.

"Don't just stand there like an idiot, idiot!" he called out to his fellow knight. "Bring the keys."

Roger rose and took a step back.

He heard one of the knights inserting the key from the other side. Violently he jolted the key inside the lock.

"What are your doing, idiot?!" the second man called. "Give that to me!"

Roger heard the metal clinching even more violently.

"It's not going in?! What devil's work is this?!" he shouted, flabbergasted.

Roger knew the reason.

He had left the skeleton key stuck inside and turned. That way it would block any key they tried to insert from the other side.

The knights started cursing him and the world as they violently tried to break the door from the inside. But the metal reinforcement made sure it kept the men inside.

Roger rushed up the stairs leading to the next floor.

The moment he sat foot on the floor, a knight came out of the room on this floor. He wasn't in armor, just some brownish surcoat.

Roger saw the knight's shocked face. But Roger recovered first from the shock and grabbed inside his bag and charged at the knight.

He pulled out a loaf of bread and shoved it into the knights mouth and brought him down until his head hit the ground, knocking him unconscious.

Roger knew better than anyone else how hard bread could become if left alone for too long.

When the knight hit the ground, Roger noticed another one inside the room that was now charging at him.

Roger immediately headed for the stairs leading up. He took a few steps but then quickly collided with the hard stone.

The knight had managed to grab his foot.

Roger quickly turned around to fend himself, but it was too late.

The knight was already on top of him and Roger could see a glimpse of the knight's fist before his head forcibly turned sideways.

A hurtful ache shot through his face. His mouth filled with blood and he was forced to spit it out.

Roger instinctively reached for his knife inside his bag. Before the knight could follow up with a second punch, Roger shoved the knife inside the knights chest.

But the second punch hit still. Another wave of pain followed. He heard the blade of the knife colliding with the ground.

When he looked at the knight's chest, he saw the reason. Beneath his surcoat was chain mail that had protected him.

The knight followed up with another punch. Roger began feeling dizzy. He could feel that he was about to pass out.

He took his arms and put them between him and the knight to fend of the incoming attacks.

After a few punches he remembered the pain of his shoulder and his arms became more wounded with each punch.

Then he felt a conquering pain in his stomach. The knight had buried his fist deep into his bowels. His lungs emptied out forcefully. Some blood left his mouth, but he could still feel the taste of iron.

He wouldn't survive for much longer, Roger realized. He waited for the next punch and fended it off. Then he spit the remaining blood in his mouth in one of the knight's eyes.

The knight stumbled backwards making Roger's legs free. He pulled his legs up and kicked the knight forcefully at his chin.

He flew backwards down the stairs and his head hit the ground, passing out like the knight before him.

Roger rose from the stairs, holding his stomach. His face, shoulder and bowels, all were in pain. But he stood up regardless.

He stumbled down the stairs, almost falling, and picked up his knife and stored it inside his bag.

Roger continued to the next floor.

He realized that he wouldn't survive another fight. He had to avoid any more from now on.

When he arrived at the upper floor, there was yet another door. He could hear another pair of faint voices from the room. But he didn't have any way to deal with them anymore. He had to trust in his luck and continued to the next floor.

This was the last one, the highest of the tower. It led to a wooden double door. The carpet went further in beneath. He laid both hands on the door and smashed them open forcefully.

He met a face that looked like it had just seen a demon entering his room.

The viscount was lying inside his chair comfortably. His desk before him was ornamented in fine carved detail befitting of the ruler of the city. The top was populated by staples of papers of varying heights.

The viscount dropped his ink pen on the spot and it left a messy mark on the document under his hand.

Before the viscount could do anything meaningful, Roger went to him and emptied the remaining contents of his oilskin on him. His face, clothes and desk were drenched in it.

In shock, the viscount tried to back away from Roger, but his chair did not aid him in his plans. It stayed where it was and started tilting backwards along with the viscount. Under his own weight he crashed onto the floor.

Roger readied his fire steel, pointing it at him visibly. When he looked at Roger again, his face filled up with fear and he desperately crawled backwards until the close wall let him no further.

The viscount's lips opened.

"Don't shout," Roger commanded him.

The viscount flinched visibly on his remarks.

"P-Persefall..." he stuttered. "How did you get in here?"

"You dug your own grave," Roger began. "Your beloved holy water that helped you prevail against a demon was your greatest weakness... apart from looking down on a Seeker, that is."

"H-holy water has a weakness, you say?" he asked in a tiny voice.

"It catches flames faster than the oil that resides on you. Your knights are burning outside, trapped in the melting armor you gave them. Want to experience yourself how it feels? I'm sure you have some armor pieces left, although I'm not sure if they'll fit," Roger said, looking at his belly.

The viscount pressed himself against the wall wanting to just pass through, but of course, that didn't happen.

"No!" he cried. "Don't kill me," he begged.

"That's not for you to decide," Roger answered coldly. "Where is she?"

The viscount's whole body shivered.

"She's not here," he told Roger. "At the church…"

Roger lightly scraped on the fire steel. Tiny sparks came out that lost their glow far before they hit the ground.

The viscount let out a shriek like a maiden in a pinch.

"I-in the cellars. Look no further than the cellars. Follow the stairs down to the lowest floor," he cried.

"I'm amazed you would try to lie in this situation. Perhaps you have no good use for your life anymore," Roger suggested. "Where are the keys?"

"I-in the drawer under my desk," the viscount whimpered, avoiding Roger's gaze and biting his teeth together.

Roger went around the desk and opened the drawer and indeed he had found a bundle of keys that seemed fitting for the lock used in cellars. He put them in his bag.

Roger went back to the desk's front and pointed the steel at the viscount.

"No! Don't kill me! My life is dear to me!" he called.

"Your comfortable life of nobility, that is," Roger said resentfully. "Does nobility not have shame? Robbing honest citizen, commanding their men to kill, charging stand owners usury for a simple space to sell their goods, …despicable!"

"Lewis Gaynesford…" Roger began, but then a small bundle on a desk near the wall caught his eyes. "Don't dare to move," he commanded the viscount.

He walked over to the desk keeping his fire steel pointed at the viscount. He looked inside the bundle. A few coins of silver and one gold were inside. He grabbed the bundle and put it in his bag.

"I'll be taking back what you robbed from me," he told the viscount.

In truth, no amount of coins in the world could pay for the suffering Lili had to endure.

The viscounts expression had changed. It was still filled with fear, but his eyes didn't look at Roger. They looked at his bag.

"Even in this moment you lust for your coins? Is there no end to your greed?" he said. "You don't have to worry about your food tomorrow since you know it will be a feast, but many of your citizens have great worries. Because you rob them of those coins. Not because you need them, just because of nobility's endless greed. And don't worry. I assure you you won't be needing those coins."

The viscount didn't answer. He just looked at Roger with pearls of sweat dripping from his round chin.

Roger walked back in front of the viscount. He readied his fire steel.

"Wait!" the viscount shouted. "I told you about the demon's location. Truthfully."

"You did," Roger answered. "But only one of your attempts was truthful."

Roger pointed the fire steel at the viscount and readied his knife.

"No! Don't kill me! Take the demon with you. Take your coins," he begged.

"I will. I assure you," Roger told him. "But don't expect

to live through this. Those who are willing to kill should be prepared to be killed."

Roger dragged the knife over the steel and ignited a starfield of glowing sparks that flew away from him in an arc.

"No! Wai—" the viscount cried unsightly. His words were cut off by the flames that engulfed him. He screamed and wounded on the carpeted floor that quickly took the flames.

If Lili hadn't been immortal, Lewis Gaynesford's men would have killed her dozens of times already. But because she was immortal, she suffered insurmountable pain.

Roger turned around and walked towards the door. He grabbed the last skin filled with river water and threw it over his shoulder.

When he had passed through the double door, his mind was occupied with the only goal he had left that tied him to this place.

Halfway down the stairs he heard an ear-shattering explosion. The water had leaked out of the skin and hit the burning oil, evaporating in an instant and scattering the oil around.

With this, the fire would spread quickly until there was nothing left of the viscount's tower. Perhaps it would serve as a starting point for the citizens to rise up against the unjust rule. But that was not of Roger's concern.

Roger descended to the next floor and quickly followed the carpet down to the next set of stairs.

But he was stopped by the sound of a door opening. He turned around in bad premonition.

He stared at a knight's face that stared back at him.

"The viscount is trapped inside his burning room. You better help to keep him alive," Roger proclaimed in an attempt of keeping the knight from chasing him to the cellars. If it came down to it, he had to fight yet another knight in his already injured condition.

But the knight didn't charge at him. He remained a few steps before the door frame.

"Are you the Seeker?" he asked.

His words felt different from the other knights.

"I am."

"Did you set the viscount's room on fire?" he continued in a calm voice.

"I did," Roger answered. "And if you don't help him, he won't make it for very long."

Shortly after Roger's answer, another knight appeared in the door frame. He showed Roger an unbelieving expression.

"I-is that the Seeker?!" he shouted. "What are you waiting for, Geoffrey?"

"Wait!" the knight at the front commanded the other, raising his hand to signal him to stop. "My name is Geoffrey Manston, what's yours?" he asked suddenly.

Roger had no idea what a knight would want with his name, but since names could be changed easily, there was no harm in returning the introduction as the manners demanded.

"It's Roger Persefall."

"He's the Seeker, Geoffrey. Let me through!" the other knight demanded, but Geoffrey Manston continued to block his path.

"The viscount is in danger," Geoffrey Manston told the other knight. "Hurry to his room, I'll follow shortly after."

Geoffrey Manston let the knight through. He gave both his fellow knight and Roger a doubting look but followed Geoffrey Manston's orders and hurried up the stairs.

"Who are you?" Roger asked the mysterious man.

"I am but a humble knight, nothing of importance," he encountered. "You're here to save the girl, aren't you? Then go and waste no time."

Roger had no idea what to make out of the man. He was a knight under the orders of the viscount, yet he told him to rescue Lili and leave the tower. He was committing treason, assisting a Seeker, an even worse felony. Assisting a Seeker would bring the same ritual upon him as designated to Seekers themselves.

The knight gave him a last look before he started walking up the stairs.

Roger had heard that they existed, people that weren't content with how Seekers were treated. He wondered if Geoffrey Manston was one of them.

Roger turned around to face the stairs and headed down.

He hurried down the stairs until he had reached the cellars again.

He went through the keys until he had found the right one and unlocked the door.

Roger hurried through the walkway. Every cell he saw on the way was empty.

He headed for the door at the end and used the keys to open it. After a loud clicking sound, he lifted the heavy metal bar.

Roger forcefully threw the bar onto the ground. The

metallic sound echoed through the cellars.

He pulled the door open. It was a heavy weight. He had to use his entire body to get it open. And then he saw her.

Chained flat on a metallic table. Her arms, neck and legs were spread out and held down by cold iron. No clothes, no dignity were remaining.

Steam raised from her naked body. A stench of blood filled the cell. Her wounds from the dozens of swords were still present. Roger clenched his teeth together. At this moment Roger hoped that the knights didn't come to the viscount's rescue. He wouldn't forgive the viscount for eternity.

Roger walked to her. Her eyes were closed. She was unconscious.

He touched one of the restraints with his finger and then rubbed his fingers together. He felt a wet sensation. All of her restraints were coated. But not only that. Her whole body was dripping with a mixture of blood and holy water.

It seemed like the holy water was fighting against her blood. It also appeared to act like acid on her body that was trying to dissolve her, but her regenerative abilities fought against it.

Roger took the keys and lifted her restraints. Each time a loud clicking sound rang in his ears. When she was freed he carefully lifted her body and carried her out of the cell like in that one night where everything began.

He walked back through the walkway, passing the countless sad cells. He went back up the stairs, each step being reminded of how light her body was. A faint crackling of the flames entered his ears coming from the upper floors. Each step it became louder. He took the last steps until he stood at the carpet that led outside. He looked upstairs. He couldn't see nor hear the knights from earlier. Everything was dead quiet. Only the sound of flames was there.

He turned around and followed the carpet until he arrived in the garden.

Roger walked through it. From there the sound of crackling flames was even more prominent. He walked further towards the gate. The sound of the blaze was replaced by voices of people.

Then with a loud crackling the blazes triumphed again. Roger looked behind him. The flames reached out of the windows and had started spreading to the lower floors. Somehow he felt like he had seen that sight before, but he couldn't remember where.

He turned back around and continued walking. The voices were now getting clearer. The flames started illuminating the outside of the garden. There were people. They were talking with voices filled with uncertainty. Their clothes looked simple. They weren't of nobility, no knights either. Those were the citizens that lived under the viscount's rule.

Roger neared the crowd. Soon, he passed the gate. Next to it lay two char-coaled armors.

Roger walked further. The talking had stopped. All attention was focused on him. He saw their faces go pale as they stared at the girl in his hands. They quietly made a path for him and he followed it until vanishing in the darkness of the faint night.

It wouldn't take long before the sun rose. It was

getting brighter by each building he passed. He followed the maze of alleys into the direction of the port.

Then he felt her moving in his arms. He looked at her.

Slowly, struggling, she opened her big eyes. Their glossiness slowly returned and she looked at him.

Tears started forming, her lips shaking.

"Roger…" she cried. "Roger…"

She cried relentlessly.

"It's alright. Everything is over."

She buried her face in his chest. Her tiny hands tried to hold onto his mantle, but they were so weak that they continued to slip off. Then she lifted her face and looked him in the eyes. Her face was close, similar to when he first met her, but his feelings were different.

"What happened?" she asked insecurely. "Why are you here? Why am I here?"

Roger smiled. "I'm sorry, I couldn't follow your words. I couldn't let you save me and then leave you behind," he told her warmly.

"I saved you?" she mumbled to herself. Then her face quickly turned away with a painful expression.

"You don't remember?"

Her lips opened and closed a few times, but no words came out. She was hesitating. Then she finally spoke up.

"I don't remember what happened. The last thing I remember was us running away," she said with a heart-breaking shiver in her voice.

How could this be? What did the viscount do to her? His anger flared up again.

"It's always this way. Whenever I touch holy water, I lose some of my last memories."

"You lose your memories?" he echoed. "How cruel," he

thought. This wasn't fair.

Then he had a shocking realization. He remembered her words at the river.

"Then… what happened at the bridge…" he began.

"I lost them as well."

How could this be? The demon girl in his hands was immortal, but her mind wasn't. To demons holy water was a liquid of death.

Another question flashed through his mind. He had a fearing premonition.

"How were you sealed?" he asked uneasily.

She looked away.

"They are gone as well," she answered sobbingly. "The last time I remember…" she began. "…we were invading the human realm and we were winning."

Roger realized what her words meant. If those were her last memories, what must they have done to her? How much of her memories did she lose?

But one thing Roger was sure of was that demons weren't as invincible as the tales said. The girl in his hands at least had been hurt many times a human could endure and had lived through many cruelties.

"Lili, rest assured now. We'll board the ship and escape the human realm. No one will give chase to the elven realm."

She wiped away her tears with her naked arms and formed a smile. She looked at Roger and nodded.

"Can we stay like this until we arrive at the port?"

"Of course," Roger answered happily.

"Say, how were I caught?" she asked all of a sudden.

Roger remembered her words. "I am glad it was you who unsealed me!" she had said to him. He was also glad he did and no one else. Even after everything that happened, right here, he didn't have any regrets.

"Don't worry. I always will remember it for the both of us," he told her.

She smiled comfortably. "Thank you for rescuing me."

Roger remembered his guilt of wanting to run away, of wanting to board the ship without her. Even if it was the curse of Seekers that drove him, it was his thoughts and his actions.

"You know, at first I felt uneasy about having a demon around. I was thinking of a place where we could part," he began. "But now I feel different. If there is one person in the world that I wouldn't mind taking along on my journey, it would be you... so I ask, will you be that person?"

He looked at her. Her mouth was wide open. His words must have surprised her. The more he thought of what he just said, the more he was convinced that he had to be drunk.

She turned her gaze to her hands she was playing around with. Her cheeks were a subtlety more red than the other parts of her face.

"I'll accompany you," she said. "If there is someone who would take the last demon along that would be you, Roger." She looked at him and showed him a big smile.

"When we've boarded the ship, I have a present for you."

"A present?" she asked, her eyes suddenly lighting up.

"A present it is!" he answered laughingly.

"Tell me! What is it? What's the present?"

"You'll see when the time comes," he told her. "See? We're there!" He pointed his eyes towards the sea.

She looked at it with wide eyes.
The morning would come soon.

Epilogue

"You know, I don't like the elves very much, but somehow I'm looking forward to go to their realm," Lili said.

She lay on the wooden planks on her stomach with her legs waving and down. Her hair covered her entire body. She was wearing her black dress. It was the only thing that was left of her clothes. But Roger thought it looked fitting on her.

Roger carefully moved the brush over her hair from the top all the way down to her legs. She was relishing every minute of it. He was glad that she liked her present.

"I guess I'm also looking forward to it. It'll be a new and interesting experience."

"I'm hungry," she said, changing the topic.

She sat up with her legs crossed, leaning against the wooden walls. She looked just like a human child that was excited to go on a journey. The only thing that gave away that she was a demon was her happily waving tail.

"I'll see what I can do," Roger said and stood up.

He felt the ship hitting the waves as his center of balance shifted. He walked to the crates at the back.

They were filled with all kinds of fruits he had never seen before. They had been lucky that the ship transported food. He had only half a loaf left and it wouldn't last for too long.

He took two colorful round fruits out of one crate. He opened his purse and took out a gold coin. He wasn't supposed to take those fruits, nor was he supposed to be on deck, hiding alongside the goods, but a piece of gold would certainly make up for it. He placed it in the box in place of the fruits and headed back to Lili.

He gave her one of the fruits and sat down next to her.

"Umm..." Lili said, holding her cheeks, her mouth covered in juice.

Roger also took a bite. His eyes widened. It was a taste he had never experienced before, somehow exciting, something new and refreshing. It was a sparkling taste that reminded him of the journey that was to come.

He closed his eyes. In the dark he could feel the spell calling from the distance. It was nearing. He wondered what the next spell had in store for him.

Certainly, after unsealing a demon, it was hard to believe that any spell after that would still surprise him. He let out a chuckle and opened his eyes again.

He looked at Lili who was devouring the fruit, her face looking like a mess. He smiled.

And so Roger and Lili drifted away from the

mainland of the human realm, leaving their chasers behind, a new journey ahead.

Made in the USA
Middletown, DE
26 January 2020

83741756R00118